Never Doubt A COWBOY

Cowboy Hero, Book 5

BARBARA MCMAHON

One

Molly Spencer almost hugged herself with glee, giddy with delight. Here she was in Mexico! A month ago she'd faced unemployment, dwindling savings and bleak prospects. Now she stood on a terrace of a two-bedroom casita overlooking beautiful Acapulco Bay.

The soft corals and pink that painted the evening sky reflected on the calm, shimmering sea. The sun sank lower in the west. Evening breezes felt cool after the sultry heat of the day, blowing in gently from the sea. The salty tang of the ocean washed across her skin in a tangible caress. Across the bay lights were blinking on in the high-rise glass and steel hotels that encircled the shore.

Her eyes delighted in the sights before her as she leaned lightly against the railing that held her at the edge. It was wonderful, heady. In her wildest imaginings she'd never pictured herself in Acapulco.

Behind her she could hear the soft murmur of her new boss talking on the phone to someone in Los Angeles. No other sounds marred the peaceful and serene setting.

Molly's eyes again skimmed the horizon, the bay, the city in the distance. It was all so magical—would she ever get tired of looking at the view? Maybe by the end of their stay, but she secretly doubted it.

She turned slowly to survey her own particular bit of Acapulco. Las Casitas D'Oro Hotel was enchanting. Built on the steep side of a hill, each room or suite opened to a private terrace, with its own private swimming-pool.

She was in a two-room suite, her bedroom to the left, her employer's to the right. The large flagstone terrace united the two rooms. A tall cinder-block wall, painted blue and white, divided their terrace from the room to their left. A half-wall to the right separated the casita from the open hillside. The large, kidney-shaped pool invited her to swim. The pool that was to be shared with Beverley, no one else.

Molly's grin threatened to split her face. This was the most wonderful place she'd ever been. And pure luck was the sole reason she was here.

She'd been a part of the huge layoff at MacInery Investing. Three weeks on unemployment, with few opportunities arising, she'd started to really worry she'd be in financial trouble when her friend Margot told her about this position–temporary personal assistant to Beverley Sampson.

She'd applied, been accepted and before she knew it, they were making plans to stay in Acapulco while Beverley worked on her latest biography.

Molly feasted her gaze on the city in the distance, memorizing every nuance, every high rise building, the strip of white sand at the edge of Acapulco Bay. She never wanted to forget this magical assignment.

He stood in the shadows and she didn't see him until he moved. Startled when she heard him, Molly spun around. He slipped easily around the wall beside Beverley's room, pausing at the gate that separated their terrace from the wild, untamed land of the hillside. Thrusting open the wooden gate, he walked boldly on to the patio as if he owned the place, a stack of fluffy blue and white towels in his arms.

He couldn't work at the resort, could he? He wore jeans, a blue shirt with sleeves rolled up to expose his forearms—and a cowboy hat. The clothes the staff wore were nothing like this. All she'd seen was the loose Mexican shirts with embroidery.

She glanced into the room where Beverley talked on the phone. Her back was to the opened door and she was clearly engrossed in her conversation. Molly looked again at the intruder. Maybe there was a legitimate reason he was here.

He stood inside the colorful blue gate, blending in with the shadows of the early evening staring at her. Was she as unexpected to him as he was to her? The light from the rooms spilled across part of the patio, making the spot where he stood outside the light seem darker, mysterious.

"Can I help you?" she asked. She was hired to help not only with transcribing the tapes Beverley made, but also to assist wherever needed.

Though probably not much over six feet tall, from Molly's diminutive five feet two he seemed to tower over her. Highlighted by the setting sun, his hat was pulled low, as if to shelter his face from the last of the sun's rays.

Unexpectedly, anticipation flared. She blinked when a curious fluttering sensation arose in the pit of her stomach.

"Who are you?" Molly asked, stepping away from the railing.

His hair was dark where she could see it beneath the hat, and he hadn't shaved for a couple of days, which enhanced his rugged masculinity. Cowboy boots looked out of place in the heat of the resort. Muscular legs, spread apart, firmly anchored him to the patio. She hoped it was only a case of mistaking their room for his own.

Molly took a breath, her eyes involuntarily drawn to his chest, trailing down to his snug jeans. Raw sex in tight jeans, she thought involuntarily and her senses tingled as awareness of his animal magnetism threatened to engulf her.

She was suddenly hot, and it wasn't only because of the instant flush when she realized where her thoughts were heading.

Compared to him, she was terribly overdressed. The hot, sultry climate required fewer articles of clothing and she still wore the suit she'd traveled in, which had been appropriate for the flight to Mexico.

She took a step closer and tried to see his face in the dim light, trying to ignore the strong desire to feast her eyes on him, schooling her features to reveal none of her thoughts, trying to ignore the sudden longing to touch him that quivered in her fingertips.

Why didn't he say something.

At the sound of her voice, he narrowed his eyes slightly as he continued to stare at her. She stood silhouetted by the setting rays of the sun. The fading light made it difficult to see her face.

"Are those our towels?" she asked again, her voice holding a hint of annoyance.

His lips twitched as he nodded and strolled over past one of the chairs, carelessly dropping the towels as he passed, staring down at her until he was almost close enough to touch.

"You just arrive?"

He looked slowly down her body again, amusement dancing in his gaze as he took in the business suit in such a hot, laid-back climate.

He wished he could see her better. With the light behind her, her face was in shadow. He let his gaze trail down to her bare feet. At least she made some concession to the heat.

"Yes, we just arrived. Did you mistake this room for yours? Or do you work here?"

He shook his head slowly, his eyes roaming freely over her trim figure. He could tell it flustered her. He wanted to laugh at her attempts to remain in control of the situation. Where had she come from, he wondered.

"If you don't work here, what are you doing?"

Molly was beginning to get annoyed. One thing she was sure of, her employer wanted privacy, not have strange men wandering around at will.

Molly grew determined to take charge. He was trespassing on her patio and she wanted him to leave.

"I'm looking at you, right now, darlin'," he said, grinning, his eyes clashing with hers. She could see the gleam of his white teeth. He shifted a little and took a step closer.

Molly frowned at his teasing tone yet when he moved she could see him better, but wasn't reassured. His eyes were still in shadow, hooded by dark brows. A two-day growth of beard covered his lean cheeks.

Yet her interest soared. He looked tired, scruffy, disheveled; but not like a vagrant, more like a man on his own, removed from daily routines, doing just as he darn well wanted.

"This isn't your room, you don't belong here, you'll have to leave," she said hoping he'd do it.

If not, what could she do?

"You're staying in these rooms? I brought some towels."

Molly had a moment of doubt. The towels looked right. The entire hotel was done in blue and white, its trademark. But the man didn't look right. None of the hotel staff she'd seen thus far had been out of the bright blue uniform of Las Casitas D'Oro.

This man looked more like Poncho Villa, wild, lawless, free. Definitely not a hotel employee out to please the guests.

He took a step closer and Molly saw him clearly in the light from Beverley's bedroom. She met his eyes with a shock. They were a light silvery gray. His skin was tanned a dusky bronze, his hair inky in the darkening sky.

"Thank you for the towels. Goodnight."

She waited, hoping her demeanor would encourage him to leave.

He smiled again. "Want me to go, do you?" His eyes danced in amusement at her as he stepped closer, placing his fists on his hips. He looked immovable.

Feeling flustered and rude, Molly none the less stood her ground. "I won't keep you from..."

From what? He'd said he didn't work for the hotel—what was he doing here?

Her eyes flickered to the short wall to her right. Beyond it was the open hillside. Wild, uncultivated land, restricted to no one. A thief could easily stalk these rooms. In and out fast. Was he here to see who had checked in? Scope out the place as it were?

"I think you'd better leave." She tried to make her voice as forceful and confident as she could.

"Your first trip to Acapulco?" he asked, ignoring her command.

"Yes, it is. And this is a private patio."

If he refused to leave, she'd make a dash to her room and call the front desk. It didn't matter that she'd hate to cause a scene practically the moment she arrived.

He smiled at that. He looked her over slowly, from head to feet, his light eyes dancing as he met her gaze again.

Molly flushed, her skin instantly warm. Suddenly convinced he saw through the trim blue skirt and silky white blouse that hugged her figure, she was startled at the awareness of her own sexuality that he raised.

She wasn't used to men like him—or the reaction of her own body. She tilted her head up to meet his gaze, standing her ground. He was the trespasser, not she. He was the one who should be embarrassed at being asked to go.

6

"Are you leaving?"

She blinked through her glasses, wishing illogically that she'd worn something soft and feminine. Wishing she'd combed her hair.

Wished he'd look at her with longing, rather than amusement.

How stupid—she was here to work, not flirt with the first man that happened by. And especially not some ruffian who hadn't seen a razor in days.

"Senorita, here I come to welcome you to this beautiful city and all you want to do is have me leave. I can show you the marvelous attractions of Acapulco, guide you to all the places tourists want to see, fill your days with wonderful sights to see, and fill your nights with warm, loving memories to dream about for years to come."

His voice was like a dark melody, piercing through to her heart. If she closed her eyes, she felt she could listen to him forever. The tone was low, smooth, sexy. The words seductive.

She shook her head, breaking the spell. What was she thinking of?

"I'm sorry, I already have plans. Thank you for the towels. Do you want a tip?"

She wanted him to go, yet he wouldn't budge.

"Are you sure you don't need a guide? How about to the beaches? I'm sure you'd look great in a swimsuit. I know where the best beaches are."

Amusement was evident in his tone. His gaze never left her face.

Was Beverley finished yet? Would she turn and see the visitor and join Molly in getting rid of him? Molly silently urged her to come outside.

Then she reconsidered. She'd been hired to help the other woman. She couldn't let her employer start out thinking Molly couldn't handle things.

Though this was getting out of hand. Molly stepped closer, a look of pure determination on her face.

"This is a private terrace and if you don't leave, I'll call the hotel security and have you removed."

She stalked over to him, intending to pass him and head for her room. If he wouldn't leave, she would. But he casually stepped between her and the door.

The terrace narrowed where he stood, the half-wall on one side, the pool on the other. She stopped abruptly, touched by a flash of fear. She didn't know who this man was, but he was between her and safety.

He was tall, strongly built. It would take very little effort on his part to sling her over his shoulder and take her into the scrub brush beyond the wall.

Molly glanced at the darkening hillside and then looked back at him, confused when she again met his gaze.

He was laughing at her.

"What is it you want?"

"Only to be of service to the lovely senorita, darlin". What do you think I want." His voice mocked, his eyes never left hers.

She was annoyed.

And a tiny bit hurt by his mocking endearment.

She was not lovely, nice looking, but a bit plain. Her glasses enabled her to see clearly, yet she often longed to be rid of them. Her dark, wavy hair was scraped back from her face in a serviceable but unremarkable french braid. She looked exactly as she was, a woman who needed to work for a living and had no money to spare for frivolous things.

She didn't need some stranger mocking her. She didn't need him here at all. Why wouldn't he leave? Her frustration grew by leaps and bounds.

"Do you want money?" she asked through gritted teeth.

"I'm insulted. Here I offer to show you the sights and you want to pay me."

He stood straight, arms falling to his side. It did not make him any less formidable. "If I wanted payment, it wouldn't be in money."

Her imagination let her know what he'd want payment in.

Her heart began pounding and she turned and walked around the pool. She'd go into her room and shut the sliding door. Maybe she'd even call hotel security.

She was halfway around when she realized he was pacing her, on the room side of the pool, slowly, steadily, matching step for step. When she reached the other end, he'd be there, cutting off her escape to her room.

She paused, feeling foolish. Were they to dance around the pool all night? Anger coursed through her. He was playing games which she didn't appreciate. One scream from her and Beverley would hear. Probably people in other rooms.

Yet she hesitated to do that.

One of the reasons Beverley Sampson had hired her was to keep her life free from interruptions while she worked on another of her biographies.

Not the primary reason, of course. Beverley had broken her wrist three weeks ago and couldn't type. She'd hired Molly as typist–temporarily until the book was finished, or the cast came off, whichever came first.

Molly took her position very seriously. She refused to be bested by this stranger. Failure to remove this man wouldn't augur well for her ability to handle other situations that might arise with the position.

And she desperately wanted to keep the job as long as she could.

When Molly stopped, the stranger did not. He continued around the pool, his eyes never leaving her. She wished for a moment he'd trip and fall into the water, but he stayed clear of the edge.

Coming up to her, he took her arm gently in one hand and slowly moved her to the railing. For a moment she thought he meant to toss her over, but he simply turned her around and motioned to the far end of the bay.

Leaning over, he put his head close to hers, pointing across the bay.

"That's where the cruise ships dock. There're none in port tonight, but there'll be one soon. They're very pretty, all in white, with flags flying and bright lights at night. Sometimes you can hear the music from the ships, if the wind's right."

He stood so close to her she felt the heat from his body. The breeze cooled her skin through her silk shirt, but the warmth from his hand permeated. She concentrated on the sights he was pointing out to her, conscious of his hand still on her arm, of the tingling sensation moving through her body as his touch energized. Conscious of his face, only inches from hers, she could see him clearly from the corner of her eye. His voice was soft, melodious, velvety in the growing darkness.

He pointed out each major hotel on La Contessa Beach by name, first the soaring Continental, then the elegant Plaza International, and the old El Presidente.

She licked her lips and tried to differentiate the various buildings, following his hand as he showed her. Her breathing grew difficult. Slowly, unobtrusively, she parted her lips to breathe better. Her heart was tripping double time and the warmth she experienced earlier was growing uncomfortable.

"It's too dark now to see," he said sadly. "I'll have to come again and point that out to you in the daytime."

"N-no." Was that her voice, so breathless? She cleared her throat and stepped back. Could she make it to her room now?

"I don't think that's a good idea," she said

"Ah, but I do, darlin". I think we should get to know each other. I can still show you the sights."

"Look, senior, I'm here to work. Not to go sightseeing, not to mingle with the–"

She stopped, appalled at her rudeness.

He laughed softly, mockingly in the dark. She could see the faint light spilling from the room gleam on his white teeth. His dark coloring seemed almost sinister in the night.

"Not mingle with the natives, eh? Well, it's early days yet, and who knows what you'll see and do here in Mexico? But I'm not Mexican."

"I know that. You speak perfect English. Are you're visiting like me?"

She was intrigued by the intruder, though she should be urging him to leave. When had the urgency to have him gone vanished?

"I'm from Texas. But I've been to Acapulco before, speak some of the language and can show you around."

She blinked, staring at him. It was evident he was brash enough to be a Texan. And a cowboy to boot. Brash, brazen, cocky as all get out.

"Wherever you're from, I don't have time to see the sights—I'm here to work."

Molly stepped casually back another foot. If she could keep him talking, she could move closer to her room and make a dash for it.

"One can work too hard," he said.

She stared up at him, her heart suffocating in its pounding. Slowly he leaned over and gently brushed her lips with his fingertips.

"Go to your room now, little one, and lock your door at night. Who knows if the wolves will come over the hill."

"Wolves?"

He shrugged and moved past her, heading for the wooden gate in the half-wall that separated the terrace from the open hillside. "Who knows? There are wolves everywhere."

"You should know that," she muttered.

His smile at her as he went through the gate made her wonder if he'd heard her.

She watched but in only seconds he was lost to the darkness. She didn't hear him move across the ground, but she knew he was gone. She felt curiously bereft.

Turning for one last look at the enchanting setting of Acapulco Bay, she slowly moved to her room. Beverley was still on the phone, so Molly decided she wasn't needed.

Switching on the lights in her room, she began unpacking the few clothes she'd brought with her. Speculating on who her visitor might have been, she put away the dresses and khaki pants. Was he staying at the resort? He didn't look the type. Most of the people she'd seen as they drove into this exclusive resort were well dressed or wearing colorful beach attire. And driving expensive cars.

Her stranger on the patio struck her as someone who scoffed at conventions, ignored rules he didn't make.

She wondered if she'd see him again. Probably not. And if he saw her in the daylight, would he be sorry? He'd been flattering in his comments, but the light was dim and kind.

Molly had no illusions. She was nice-looking, but not the type to inspire wild fantasies in men. She didn't know how to flirt or dress to entice. Life hadn't been easy and she was very careful with her money. She wouldn't be caught with nothing the way her mother had been.

This job with Beverley Sampson was a gift from heaven. Molly smiled at her good fortune as she hung up the last of her cotton dresses, put the suitcase in the bottom of the spacious closet. Her old company had eliminated so many job that day.

She was so glad Margot had learned of the writer's accident and her need for a typist.

Beverley had written over a dozen biographies of famous people. She was well known in literary circles and had been unexpectedly left unable to complete her current manuscript when she'd broken her wrist.

She made it clear at the interview it was a temporary assignment, but when the job ended, she'd give a glowing reference. Molly was thrilled to have the job. Not only would she be bringing in money, she also had an all-expense paid trip to Acapulco.

Beverley planned to stay in Mexico for at least a month, to finish the draft of her latest manuscript before sending it to her publishers.

When Beverley told Molly they'd be a month in Mexico, Molly had expected a small house or apartment on a back-street, something inexpensive.

Instead, they had two rooms at one of Mexico's most expensive resorts. She'd never dreamed of such a place and delighted in each new discovery.

However, when Molly went to bed that night it wasn't the excitement of her new job or the luxuries of Las Casitas D'Oro that danced in her mind, but the image of mocking gray eyes, broad shoulders and dark hair.

She smiled wistfully, wishing she might see him once again, wondering who he was. Why had he delivered the towels? Was it an excuse to check out the new arrivals? She hoped he wasn't a thief.

Two

Molly awoke early the next morning, anticipation welling up. She was in Mexico. Starting a new job in a wonderful location. Anxious to greet the day, she hurried through dressing, donning white cotton trousers and a bright yellow top. Brushing her hair back, she quickly braided it into a serviceable braid. Her thick hair felt hot and heavy in the warm morning, but at least the braid kept most of it off her neck.

Sliding open her door, she stepped out on to the patio. Involuntarily her eyes were drawn to the gate where the mysterious visitor from last night had disappeared. Illogically, she was disappointed he wasn't there, though there was no reason to expect him.

Glancing at the beauty before her, she walked casually over to the half-wall, sweeping her gaze across the open hillside. She saw only wild brush, rocks and an occasional burst of yellow or red wildflowers. There was no path, no indication that anyone had walked across the ground last night.

Where had he come from, and where had he gone? The questions teased her mind as she forced herself to look across to the wrought-iron railing to the view she so loved last night. The sky was clear and blue. The sun's rays sparkled on the glittering high-rises lining the distant beach, glistened on the deep blue water.

Molly remembered the mysterious stranger's touch as she gazed over sights he'd pointed out last night. She could almost feel his fingers on her arm, the warmth of his breath near her face, the sensuous touch of his fingers on her lips. It was almost as if he were there.

She turned slightly, expectantly, disappointed to find she was still alone.

Glancing over her shoulder, she saw the door to Beverley's room was still closed.

A large tray with covered baskets, a coffee carafe and two dainty cups and saucers rested on one of the small tables beside the pool. Molly smiled at the breakfast service.

Rolls, croissants and pastries nestled in the baskets, still warm in their cozy. The coffee was hot and fragrant. She filled a cup and took a croissant.

Wandering back to the railing, she munched as she gazed over the view, her mind drifting, her eyes enjoying the beauty of the scene. She knew she was there to work, but the perks when not working couldn't be any better.

The sound of the sliding door drew her attention and Molly turned to greet her employer. Beverley Sampson emerged from her room the way a bird might emerge from a nest, looking around her, her eyes dark and darting hither and yon.

"Good morning, Molly, how did you sleep? I always sleep poorly the first night in a new place. Though I wouldn't call this a new place—I've stayed here many times before. Still, I guess it takes some adjustment to get used to a different bed from the one you're used to. Did you sleep well? How do you like the view? No matter what room I get here the view is always the same and I know I can count on it to be spectacular."

Beverley smiled vaguely at Molly, obviously expecting no answer, as she hurried over to the rolls and coffee. She was tiny, barely five feet tall, but bubbly and lively. Molly thought she had

15

to be in her fifties, but her hair was light brown and touched up so Molly wasn't sure.

She'd been a shock to Molly when she began working for her two weeks ago. She'd expected a writer to be quiet and thoughtful.

Beverley was just the opposite, lively, talkative, given to blurting things out without thought, and without fear of consequences. Molly had never been around anyone quite like her and found it disconcerting at times. She hoped she'd get used to her new boss soon.

This morning, however, she merely smiled and went to sit in the chair near the table.

"I slept fine, thank you. The croissants are delicious," she said, offering the basket to Beverley, settling back to enjoy breakfast on the sunny patio. "Do you need help?"

Beverley's broken wrist made it difficult for her to eat at times. Molly was ready to assist however she could.

"I can manage croissants. Mmm, I always like breakfast here. No matter what time I get up, it's waiting. I often wonder if they put it out the night before, but then how could the rolls stay so warm? Don't you love the coffee? It seems richer than what we have in the States, don't you think? I love it, especially with milk."

Beverley took a roll and turned to look at the view, a pleased expression on her face. Molly watched her uncertainly, not sure of what her next duties would be. Beverley had been somewhat vague when explaining her assignment to her.

"I want someone to type for me until my wrist heals and to put up with my thinking out loud. Maybe do some research for facts, dates, and so on. Help keep away the locals when in Mexico. So often they want more time from me than I can afford to give. Do you speak Spanish? No, well, never mind. I speak it quite well. I grew up on the border and knew as much

Spanish as English when I started school. Any questions?"

Molly smiled, remembering her interview. Beverley had done most of the talking, Molly hardly able to get a word in. In spite of that, Beverley had been satisfied and hired her.

So far Molly found transcribing the manuscript fascinating.

"I want to go into Acapulco for a few things this morning," Beverley said, looking at Molly. "Want to come along? You can browse around, shop a little. You might not get out for a few days once we back on the book. Did you bring cooler clothes?" She looked at Molly's trousers. "It gets very hot here and humid. I don't like the air-conditioner running all the time. You should get some things that will be cooler. I always wear shorts and light tops when working."

Molly nodded. Knowing she'd be able to pick up a few things for less money in Mexico than in Los Angeles, she'd purposely not bought anything special for the trip. And LA got hot enough. She had enough to tide her over. Shed allocated a little money for purchases.

But not all of her savings. It was wise to have some in reserve. One never knew what the future would bring and Molly wanted to be prepared no matter what.

Beverley rented one of the colorful blue and white jeeps from the hotel. She insisted on Molly driving since her injured wrist precluded her driving with a stick shift.

"And when you have time off if I don't want it, you can use it whenever. You can go exploring around the area or shopping or to the beach."

The ride down the hillside from the hotel was hair-raising from Molly's point of view. The jeep had no doors so she cinched her seat belt tight. Keeping the car at what she thought would be a safe speed, nevertheless felt like she was a race driver with the asphalt rushing by all the more noticeable without the protection of doors.

Beverley exclaimed how much fun it was acting as though she were on a thrill ride at an amusement park.

Molly drove straight for town as Beverley chatted non-stop. She pointed out the various sights along the drive to Molly, indicating where they'd turn off to use the beach club belonging to the hotel, indicating where friends of hers lived, and where Molly should drive one day to see the other side of the hill, the rural setting home to Acapulco natives.

Breathing a sigh of relief once in the city limits, Molly was pleased to find a parking garage near one of the high rise hotels and pulled in at Beverley's direction.

"Exciting place, Acapulco. I love it. I come here as often as I can. Writing can be done anywhere, so why not at a place I love? I have some errands and know you'd like to look around. We'll meet for lunch at one. Right here, don't be late. I don't like people to be late," Beverley said.

With a friendly, bird-like smile, Beverley jumped down from the jeep and scurried down the main street.

Molly watched with startled eyes as her employer disappeared from view. She was on her own.

Well, she hadn't expected that.

There was nothing to lock, so she pocketed the keys and stepped out to go exploring.

She looked around the busy street when she reached the sidewalk, the crowds spilling into the stores and shops. Feeling somewhat guilty that she wasn't working, she slowly headed toward what looked like a major thoroughfare.

When she reached the main street she saw it lined with shops of all sizes displaying their colorful wares in large windows and on racks lining the pavement. Everything imaginable seemed available. She began walking, watching the people, window-shopping, absorbing the foreign sights and sounds.

Colorful ponchos, decorated sombreros and wooden figurines were set up to lure the tourist. The friendly shopkeepers standing in the doorways greeted everyone and urged them to try their shop.

Most of the people she passed on the street were visitors—scantily dressed, bathing suits being the attire of choice, cover-ups optional. Short shorts, skimpy tops, and bare feet were everywhere.

Molly began to feel positively overdressed in her white cotton pants and cotton top.

Spanish was loud and rampant around her as exuberant Mexicans greeted each other in passing and stopped to talk. She also caught snatches of German, French and another language she couldn't guess. Once or twice she heard English.

"Obviously you've come to shop so you can fit in with the rest of the tourists." A warm, familiar voice sounded over her left ear.

Molly spun around, and there he was—her mysterious stranger from last night. Only inches away.

He'd shaved, she noticed immediately. She gazed at him startled to find him as compelling in the bright sunlight as he'd been last night. He wore a cowboy hat, blue shirt and the ubiquitous jeans. She looked up, suddenly conscious of every inch of him her eyes had tracked from his long legs to the expanse of his chest.

"Know me again?" he asked.

She nodded, wondering what it would feel like if he kissed her.

Shocked at that thought, she met his gaze, praying he couldn't read minds.

His eyes laughed down at her, and she look away quickly, flustered. She was acting like a teenager with a crush on some jock. Was the heat to blame?

Taking her arm, he turned her back toward the direction she'd been going and fell into step beside her. She felt his warm, hard fingers through the thin cotton of her sleeve, firm against her arm, causing the most peculiar constriction to her breathing.

She looked straight ahead, but saw nothing, only a swirl of color.

She chanced a glance at her companion, noting again his broad shoulders, bronzed in the morning sun. His jeans were frayed along the bottom, his boots scuffed and dusty. His legs were long and muscular. He made her feel feminine and protected.

She wished she knew him better. Maybe they could do some sightseeing together. She'd better watch where her thoughts were leading. Was this what Mexico did to people, make them forget all their inhibitions? She didn't know this man. She peeked up at his face and found his eyes staring down at hers.

"I like looking at you, too," he said audaciously.

She stopped and faced him, jerking her arm from his hand.

"I never said that." she protested strongly, guilty because she did like looking at him. But he didn't need to know that.

He smiled. "You can't keep your eyes off me."

"Only because I can't believe you'd be downtown dressed like that."

His hair was shaggy, almost to his broad shoulders, yet on him it looked good. In fact, everything about him looked good. Molly found him disturbingly sexy.

He looked at her shirt, long cotton trousers, his gaze doing strange things to Molly's equilibrium. She remembered his comment from last night and the feelings she'd had. Her pulse fluttered. She was already warm, growing hotter and sticky in the humid air as a vague anticipation pulsed through her.

That was the problem–the weather was hot and humid. It

had nothing to do with the man standing before her.

She turned away and looked at the others on the street with real attention. The revealing bikinis worn by the tourists were mere scraps of color, barely within decency. The men wore shorts or swimming-trunks. Here and there a bright shirt covered sun-reddened skin, but, for the most part, the tourists were scantily clothed.

She spotted the residents of Acapulco, however. They were more properly dressed, the men in cotton trousers and white shirts, the women in bright skirts and loose-fitting blouses.

She glanced back, surprised to find his eyes firmly on her. With all the lovely women flaunting their tanned bodies, it was a wonder he'd spare a second glance in her direction.

She pushed her glasses firmly in place and tilted her head a little. Just what did he want?

"I'm looking for some shorts, not souvenirs," she admitted. She planned to augment her wardrobe with local clothes suitable to this hot climate.

"And a swimsuit?" he asked, his eyes flicking down her body, back to her eyes. "You should get your hair cut—it's too hot here for long hair."

"I'm here to work, not play. I can put it up if it gets too hot."

Actually the thought of it piled on top of her head sounded good. The thick braid was hot against her neck and back.

"So you say. Come on, darlin, splurge a little."

He steered her into one of the open-fronted shops. Racks of colorful blouses, T-shirts, beach wear cover-ups and shorts of every hue ranged deep into the interior. The pinks and blues were vibrant, the yellows deep and bright. Green, purple, rose, the colors swirled into a kaleidoscope of color.

Molly looked eagerly at the displays, noting the inexpensive cost. She could buy a few outfits and maybe a swimsuit. She'd brought an old black one-piece which she hadn't worn much. Beverley had said they'd have a pool. Normally she didn't usually have much time for going to a beach. Here, even if she only had a few minutes each day, she could use the pool.

A saleswoman approached Molly, a polite smile on her face. When she saw the man beside her, her smile broadened, and the woman picked up her pace. Her eyes never left the face of Molly's companion.

Molly glanced at him again. He was something to draw the eye. She scanned the store quickly, noticing several women watching him as they pretended to examine clothes. That feeling of awareness grew within her.

He was more man than she knew how to handle. Gorgeous to boot. No wonder all the women were watching him. He was the type that dreams were made of.

Dreams for others, not for her. She knew her limitations. She wouldn't get tied down with some Adonis with no money and no future as her mother had. She knew the heartache and despair such actions could cause.

Molly would be very cautious before letting herself be drawn to a man, no matter how good-looking.

"Buenos dias, senorita, may I help you?" the sales clerk said when she reached Molly.

"I'd like to look around first," Molly said, gesturing at the colorful racks.

"Of course. In the back there are stalls for trying on the clothes."

She nodded to Molly, her eyes on the tall bronzed man, her smile seductive and welcoming.

Molly felt a prick of jealousy. Surprised at herself, she frowned and moved away, going slowly through the shop, examining the shorts, skirts, and festive sun dresses. She loved the bright colors and the casual, flowing lines.

Her budget was limited, but she should be able to find something to suit her.

"Try this."

A pretty hot-pink swimsuit was dangled before her. "The color will look good on you."

"There's not enough to it—how would you know?" she protested. The suit was a two-piece, and looked small enough for a child.

"Do you see any others that are more to your liking?" His eyes always laughed at her.

Molly was flustered. In truth, all the suits were skimpy.

"Maybe another store," she said.

Without a word, he took her arm and propelled her to the back, gently shoving her into one of the stalls.

"I never knew a woman yet who didn't at least like to try things on."

He dropped the suit in her hands and yanked the cloth curtain closed.

Molly frowned. She normally didn't do anything like this. Who was he?

And just how many women had he gone shopping with to know they liked to try things on?

Suddenly feeling reckless and daring, she stepped out of her clothes and pulled on the suit.

"I can't wear this," she said as she saw herself in the mirror.

The curtain slid open and he met her eyes in the mirror, then dropped to study her reflection. The bright pink of the suit deepened the pink in her cheeks, making the pale skin of her body seem whiter. The bikini-top plunged low, the swell of her breasts rounded above the fabric. The pants were low-cut, scarcely giving her decency. Her stomach was flat, her hips flared and her legs tapered beneath the satiny material.

Smoldering gray eyes clashed with hers in the mirror, as he

drew a finger across the top of the bikini pants along the back. Molly's breath caught in her throat as she jumped away.

"You need a tan, darlin'". The suit's perfect."

He felt the blood rushing in his ears. She was a knockout in that skimpy suit. Who knew her body was so seductive when she wore the slacks and shirt she'd had on. Or the business attire from last night.

His visit to Acapulco was looking up–if he could convince her to let him show her the sights.

Molly felt the blood pound through her body, thunder in her ears as she gazed back, his touch sending erotic shocks through her. She was drowning in the smoky gray of his eyes, her own will lost as she stared in stunned awareness of his maleness.

He moved first, bringing up a handful of colorful tops and skirts.

"Try these." He tossed them over the small bench along the side. "This'll go good with the suit." He thrust a loose white cover-up into her hand. Lace traced the edges, ribbons tied it closed.

Anxious to cover her body from this disturbing man, Molly put it on. It was frilly, frivolous and feminine–and totally impractical. She loved it.

"It's pretty. You look pretty, soft, feminine." His voice was low, charming, sexy.

Her eyes flew to his, startled to find them narrowed as he looked at her. She could feel the pull of attraction as if he'd reached out and touched her. She couldn't look away. She couldn't move.

Ever since she'd been on her own she'd striven to look cool and sophisticated and professional. Now this man, this stranger, had her all mixed up. All of her training and practical nature fled—for an instant she longed to be pretty, for him.

She'd taken off her glasses to try on the suit. He was slightly blurry in the mirror, but she was afraid to turn to face him—couldn't drag her eyes away from his, even to turn around.

"This stuff must cost the earth," she said stiffly, still caught in his gaze. She longed to purchase it, wear it for him, knowing it would be a monumental mistake.

"This is Mexico—nothing costs the earth here."

He smiled at her and reached up to undo her french braid. Molly couldn't move. She stared at the two of them in the mirror as if she were watching two other people. Surely neither of them was her.

He spread her hair across her shoulders, spilling it over to frame her face, trailing his fingers through its softness. With a sudden move, he scooped it up, exposing the delicate lines of her neck.

"You should get it cut," he said again. "Try on the other things. See what you want and we can go to the beach."

"I can't." The depth of her disappointment caught her by surprise. "I'm meeting my employer for lunch. I can't be late."

"We can go for a while, if you hurry." He let her hair slowly fall through his fingers and closed the curtain.

Molly tried the rest of the clothes on. All were delightfully feminine and pretty. If she could afford them, she'd love to have them all. So much for planning to be prudent.

Tell Harden leaned against the wall, crossing his arms across his chest and tried to wait patiently while she tried on the clothes. He could picture her in that bikini and his blood heated again. He couldn't wait until they went swimming. He'd find an excuse to touch her, feel that soft skin, maybe run his fingers through hair silky hair again.

"Put your suit back on for the beach," he called to her.

He wanted to urge her to hurry, but he knew that'd never happen. She was nothing like the women he normally spent time with. She was cautious and deliberate.

He smiled remembering last night. He checked the clock he spotted near the cash register. It was mid morning. They'd have time at the beach before she had to go to lunch–if she hurried.

Molly put on the bikini and then pulled her white trousers and yellow top over it. She was not yet ready to stroll the streets in only her swimsuit no matter what the rest of the inhabitants did.

She left the shirt open so the proprietor wouldn't think she was trying to steal the suit. Pulling her hair back into a pony-tail and firmly replacing her glasses, she looked more like herself. Taking a deep breath, she turned to leave.

When she pushed open the curtain, her companion smiled mockingly. "Now don't you feel more like you fit in here?"

His gaze told her he knew why she was buying the suit. It had nothing to do with the others on the street.

Only between themselves.

She flushed at his look, tilting her chin, wishing she could come back with a comment to set him in his place.

"I don't know if I want to go to the beach with you," she said, lying through her teeth.

She couldn't wait.

The comment obviously missed setting him in his place. He ignored her and again took her arm, leading her to the cash register. Speaking rapidly in Spanish, he gestured to the clothes. The saleswoman took them and began folding and placing in a large bag, all the while flirting with the man while she totaled the bill.

Molly watched, fascinated. The exchange went on for several minutes. Molly saw him smile at the woman, obviously not averse to using his charm to aid in the negotiations. The man was a born flirt. She needed to remember that.

The saleswoman nodded, smiling broadly and reached out

shake his hand. He smiled deep into her eyes, holding her hand a shade longer than necessary Molly noticed with a twinge. She cleared her throat.

Mocking eyes swung to her, and he told her the cost of the goods, watching her as she pulled out the money to pay for the clothes.

"They're so cheap," she murmured as she counted the unfamiliar currency.

"Your amigo, he bargain good," the woman said, smiling again at the man.

Molly looked up at him in surprise. "Can you do that?"

He chuckled at her expression. "It's expected. Never pay the asking price."

Molly gathered her packages and moved towards the pavement, unsure just what to do. Would he expect her to go with him to the beach? She wanted to, yet was afraid. She didn't know this man at all.

"Where did you learn to speak Spanish so well?" she asked, reluctant to push the issue.

"Grew up in Texas. I have lots of friends on both sides of the border."

"Do you still live there?" she asked, her eyes carefully ahead. She wanted to know more about this man.

He paused a moment. She realized she didn't even know his name. Didn't he want to talk about himself? Was this a pick up nothing more?

She looked at him, but he was watching the traffic. It was hectic as the cars barreled along, uncaring of the pedestrians who tried to cross to the beach.

"Come on, we'll head to the beach as soon as we find a break in the traffic. Yes, I still live there."

When the light changed a block away, he guided her through the cars until they reached the other side and to the sparkling white sand.

He looked down at her. "And where do you live?"

"I live in Los Angeles."

Disappointment touched her. He didn't live anywhere near her. Once her visit here was over, she'd never see him again. The thought brought her up suddenly. She wasn't sure she'd even see him after today.

"What do you do?" she asked.

"What do you think, dressed like this? I'm a cowboy, darlin'."

He smiled a lazy smile at her, his eyes amused as they watched her expression.

She didn't know much about cowboys, but she knew they were never rich. And if she became involved with anyone she wanted him to have money. Not be rich, necessarily, just comfortably off so money'd never be a worry.

Though she doubted this man let anything worry him.

Good grief, she wasn't getting involved with this man. She'd just run into him on the street, spoken with him briefly last night.

"Wish I knew what you're thinking. Your expressions are fascinating." His voice broke into her thoughts.

"I don't even know your name," she said in surprise.

"Tell Hardin, Molly Spencer."

"How did you know mine?"

Had she told him last night?

He grinned and took her bags.

"Come on, the sand and sea are waiting and your time's short."

There were scores of sun-worshipers already sprawled on the soft white sand. Scattered the length of the beach were conical thatched umbrellas offering spots of shade on the hot, sunny day. The water of the large bay was a deep blue, the small surface waves danced in the sunlight, reflecting the sun's rays like a million diamonds. The sky was a light blue, clear and limitless. On the opposite side of the bay she could see her hotel marching up the hillside.

Molly shrugged out of her shirt and trousers and sat on the warm sand. The air was slightly salty, clean and fresh, blowing lightly in from the sea.

Tell took off his jeans, revealing a swim suit beneath. Pulling his shirt over his head, he sat beside her on the sand.

"This is great, so pretty and relaxing," she said studying the water, the beach.

"It's why people came to Acapulco," he murmured, lying back on the sand using his hat as a pillow, closing his eyes.

Molly studied him as he lay in the sun, his body big next to hers. His shoulders were broad and muscular his chest rising and falling slowly as he breathed.

She looked at his face, his chin firm, his nose strong, his eyebrows dark and arched. The lashes lay on his cheeks, dark and thick. How unfair, she thought, that someone as masculine as he should have such beautiful lashes. She eyed him speculatively.

Molly took a deep breath and looked away, confused by the sudden desire to feel his warm skin beneath her fingers. She clenched her fists, trying to dispel the tingling yearning in her hands. Was she getting sunstroke?

"Are you on vacation?" she asked desperately.

"Yep."

"Staying at Las Casitas D'Oro?"

He opened one eye and looked over to her. "Nope. That's for rich people."

"Where are you staying?"

"Camping out."

Was he too poor to even afford a room at one of the

cheaper places, Molly wondered, dismayed.

"How did you get here?" she asked.

He rocked up on one elbow and looked up at her, his eyes narrowing against the sun's brightness.

"What is this, twenty questions?"

"I was just curious about you, that's all."

"Next you'll want to know if I'm married."

A sudden panic gripped her. "Are you?"

He shook his head, that heart-stopping lazy grin back on his face. "Are you?"

"No."

She looked out over the water. There'd never been anyone special in her life. She hadn't had time for anyone. She had her own way to make, her own future to plan for, and no time for meeting men and falling in love.

Once she felt secure, once she had money in the bank, a safety net, then she'd see about finding someone to love, someone to share her life with.

But not yet, she had too much at stake to get sidetracked by falling for some guy. Especially one with no money.

Tell reached out a finger and traced it from her shoulder down her arm to her wrist.

Molly shivered beneath his touch, her nerve-endings almost sparking beneath his finger. She yearned for more.

She was unbearably conscious of his body only inches from hers. The hot sun beat on her shoulders and her legs, but the trail his finger left rivaled its heat. Her heart skipped faster, her breathing became constricted.

"Want to go to dinner with me tonight?" His voice was low and even.

"I don't know. Unlike you, I'm not here on vacation. I'm working."

"doing?"

"Assistant to a writer. I type her manuscript, organize notes, help with research. I'm new at it, so don't know yet what my schedule will be."

"You must get some free time."

"Yes, but I don't know when yet."

"If you can go to dinner, call Miguel at the concierge's desk at your hotel—he'll be able to contact me. Just let me know."

"Okay," she said daringly, hoping she had the time free, yet wondering if she'd be doing the right thing. She'd just met him.

While she was totally entranced by this man, and wouldn't mind spending some of her free time with him while in Acapulco, work came first.

She glanced at her watch, startled to see how late it was. "I have to be going. I'm supposed to meet my boss at one."

"We haven't even gone into the water," he said.

"Sorry, duty calls. I need to meet my boss for lunch." She scrambled around to get dressed.

"Do you like your job?" he asked as she brushed off the sand before donning her street clothes.

"I like it so far. Beverley Sampson's my boss—have you heard of her?"

"Oh, yeah." Tell nodded, rising to stand beside her as he shook the sand from his clothes and put them back on.

The casual way he had about him had her wishing she was more comfortable with her own sexuality, wishing she could carry it off as effortlessly as he did. It took all her will-power to keep from looking at him, from feasting her eyes on his strong body.

He didn't speak as they walked back to the jeep and Molly began to wonder if he'd changed his mind about dinner. When she saw Beverley waiting at the edge of the parking garage, she pointed her out to Tell.

"That's Beverley there, my boss."

Molly waved, but Beverley was looking straight ahead and didn't see her.

He paused, turning partly away from Beverley and handed Molly her bags.

"Remember, let Miguel know if you can go."

"I will."

She didn't want to say goodbye. She wanted to stay with him, to forget her job, forget why she was in Acapulco. Appalled at where her thoughts were leading, she smiled shyly and turned towards her employer, hurrying to meet her.

She remembered what Beverley had said about punctuality. At least this time, she was a couple of minutes early.

"Stay away from the likes of him," Beverley said when Molly drew near. She watched Tell Hardin walking away down the sidewalk. "He's not for someone like you."

"Do you know him?" Molly asked, surprised by her employer's outburst.

"I'd say—trouble from the day he was born. What did you buy?"

Molly showed her the clothes in the bag, explaining as they walked to one of the open restaurants lining the beach. It was crowded inside, but Beverley was able to get a choice table. Seated on the seaward side, overlooking the beach and water, Beverley ordered a seafood salad and Molly followed her employer's lead, wishing the whole while that it was a tall Texan opposite her instead of her new boss.

How did Beverley know him? Dare she ask?

Three

Lunch was pleasant on the shaded veranda overlooking the wide sandy beach. No more was said of Tell Hardin, though dozens of questions crowded Molly's mind.

Did Beverley know Tell personally? Had they met here in Acapulco? What was his reputation? And what kind of trouble had he been since the day he was born? She must have known him a long time to say something like that.

Molly didn't feel comfortable enough with her new boss to inquire about someone she'd just warned her off from, but she longed to know the answers. Could she ask Tell herself?

Molly'd only been working with Beverley for two weeks. When Beverley searched for an assistant after she'd broken her wrist, she'd emphasized her practice of traveling and working while in foreign countries, cautioning Molly that they could be gone a month or more.

"That way I can satisfy my desire to travel, yet still keep working on current projects. Sometimes I combine working on one project with research on another. How does working in Mexico sound to you?" Beverley asked at the interview.

"Wonderful," Molly had replied quite truthfully. She'd never been outside Los Angeles in all her twenty- four years. Optimistically, she'd obtained a passport several years ago. But the chance to visit a different country hadn't happened.

To travel to Acapulco within a few days of starting work seemed like a dream come true.

She'd been delighted with Beverley's job offer. The writer paid top wages to compensate for the inconvenience of traveling.

Molly, who thought traveling was wonderful, couldn't believe her good fortune at top wages to boot.

Carefully planning to save a good portion, knowing this was a temporary position, she still had quite enough for her modest needs.

She hoped the job market would open up a bit by the time she finished the assignment with Beverley.

As she ate, listening with half an ear to Beverley's chatter, she envisioned the dancing gray eyes of Tell.

Regretfully she pushed his image aside. Not for her a cowboy unable to afford even a hotel room. Not for her the sexy, smoky gray eyes, narrowed in assessment as he studied her in her bright bikini.

At the memory, her skin flushed slightly and her heartbeat sped up. The lazy way he'd run his finger down her arm at the beach caused her to gaze out over the white sands, searching for his bronzed body, looking at all the tall male forms walking or lounging on the sand.

Had he picked up another woman by now? Someone out for fun and games and not tied to a job that'd take up most of her waking hours.

She didn't like the thought of him seeing someone else. Yet how dumb was that. They'd just met and not in what she'd call normal circumstances.

And she'd been warned away by her new boss. Which made her curiosity spike. What kind of woman was for him?

No matter how hard she tried she couldn't erase his image: it hovered before her, tantalizing her. She longed to forget she'd ever met him, longed for the excitement of her new job to consume her, not the unbidden thoughts of the tall, rugged male that wouldn't be banished.

She lightly licked her lips, wondering what kind of trouble he was, besides a decided threat to her own sanity.

Beverley began work in earnest when they returned to their casita. Dictating passages, requesting verification of quotes and sources, she paced her large bedroom as she reeled off names, dates and events into her recorder.

Molly worked at the desk in her own room, transcribing the dictation directly into the computer. She couldn't keep up with Beverley's rate of dictation. She hoped the writer didn't keep this pace every day.

The sun had set when Beverley entered the room and handed Molly another tape.

"Finish that tape you're on and this one in the morning. I'll check some of the other sources before continuing, so you should be able to catch up. You type fast, but I'll need to see the manuscript to know if you're as good in the accuracy department."

"I can finish up tonight," Molly said quietly.

The dinner hour was long past. She kept her eyes on her work, refusing to remember she'd been asked out, refusing to think of what might have happened if she'd been able to meet Tell for dinner, if they had been alone, the two of them.

"No, no, no. Order something from room service and enjoy the evening on the patio. You might want to swim; the water will be warm after today's heat. I'm going to take a hot bath and read. It's relaxing for me. And the next best thing to swimming which I can't do until this wrist heals. I'll put on the air-conditioner and shut all the windows and be all by myself.

You'll be all right on your own, won't you? See you after breakfast."

Beverley smiled and left. A moment later Molly heard her drawing closed the sliding door and pulling her curtains.

Molly believed writers were eccentric. Beverley was mercurial at least. She hoped they'd continue to get along. But to close herself up in an air-conditioned room when she could have dinner on the patio overlooking Acapulco Bay seemed really odd.

Molly couldn't wait to stand by the railing and see the city lights come on.

She ordered a light salad and rolls than switched off her light, wandering out into the balmy night. The sparkling lights of Acapulco surrounded the bay, reflecting on the calm sea, a thousand lights to rival the stars in the clear night sky.

The air was warm, scented with the sweet fragrance of night-blooming jasmine. It caressed her skin like a lover's touch. She smiled in quiet happiness.

"No dinner, huh?" Tell's silky voice spoke softly from the far corner. Surprised, Molly swiveled towards him, straining to see him in the dim light.

She darted a nervous glance at Beverley's room, relieved to see the curtains were still drawn.

"What are you doing here?" Molly whispered, moving slowly over to where he sat stretched out on one of the pool's loungers.

"When you didn't call Miguel, I decided to come see why not. I saw. You were busy working. So I waited."

"You shouldn't be here."

Her voice was low—she didn't want Beverley coming to investigate, didn't want her finding Tell here after warning her against him.

Tell ignored her and stood up slowly, peering down at her

in the dark.

"So, have you eaten?"

"I ordered dinner from room service. They said it'd be about forty- five minutes."

"Time for a swim, then. Do you still have your swimsuit on beneath those things?"

"Yes, but I don't think--"

Molly's voice stopped abruptly when Tell reached out and began unbuttoning her blouse. His fingers were warm as they brushed lightly against her skin, his eyes intent on the task. Slowly he pushed each button through its hole and the soft yellow cotton spread away from her, exposing the bright pink bikini.

She swallowed hard, mesmerized by his actions. She should stop him, protest, but she felt drugged, unable to move, unable to breathe. She could only look at Tell in the dim light and tremble as his fingers brushed against her heated skin.

Slowly he opened her shirt and gently pushed it off her shoulders. Molly's insides began to melt and her knees grew decidedly weak. She'd never had a man undress her before—it wreaked havoc with her senses.

He shrugged out of his shirt a moment later. His strong chest was before her, tantalizing her with the mat of dark hair she longed to tangle her fingers in. She swallowed hard, tried to move her eyes from the enticing expanse.

When his fingers reached her waistband, slipping inside to work the fasteners, she stepped back, her hands pulling his free.

"I can manage," she said huskily, turning slightly away, forcing her fumbling fingers to move. She stepped out of her slacks, glad for the darkness. She was extremely conscious of how much of her was revealed by the daring bikini.

Tell toed off his boots and shucked his jeans, revealing a tight black swimsuit. He had a beautifully shaped body, wide shoulders, long legs and flat stomach. She could stare at him for hours.

Tell dived cleanly into the water, surfacing at the far edge. "It's great."

Molly placed her glasses on the table by the pool, flung caution to the wind and followed. When she broke the surface, she felt alive as never before. The water was warm and silky against her skin, refreshing after the heat of the day and the hours spent over the computer.

"It is great. I can't believe I'm here."

She smiled, dragging her hair out of her face. She'd worn the pony tail all afternoon, but released her hair when she'd ordered dinner.

"Not everyone has their own private pool," Tell said whimsically.

They swam for a while, lazily back and forth in the warm water, the only light cast by the stars and the reflections from the far distant hotels.

When Molly had enough, she swam to the stairs and slowly climbed out of the water. The night air was only a few degrees cooler and caressed her skin like a lover.

She drip dried as she walked to the railing to enjoy the view. Wringing her hair, she left it hanging down her back, a damp cloak against her cooled skin.

Tell left the pool and joined her, in his hands hibiscus blossoms from the side of pool. Carefully he tucked a red one behind her ear; the pale pink one he gently tucked in the valley between her breasts.

Molly looked up, startled, her heart beating heavily at his touch. She'd never been touched so much by a man, moreover one she scarcely knew. It was unsettling, exciting and disturbing.

"Beverley said I shouldn't associate with you," she blurted out.

He raised one eyebrow, his face amused. "Oh, why's that?"

Molly wished she'd not spoken. She shrugged.

He reached for her arms, his fingers holding her firmly as he looked down at her, his thumbs moving against the soft satin of her inner arm.

"What exactly did she say?"

"She said to stay away from you. That you were trouble since the day you were born."

"Now how would she know that?" he asked softly, a look of pure amusement on his face.

"Probably recognizes your type," she snapped, tired of him laughing at her all the time. Couldn't he ever take her seriously?

"And what is my type, darlin'?" His voice was dangerously low, very calm. But Molly was warned by it.

"I don't know. Are you trouble?"

"Depends."

He let her go and moved to lean against the railing, the twinkling lights of Acapulco behind him. Molly's eyes were used to the dim light surrounding them. She could see, though everything was blurry. She didn't want to put on her glasses. She didn't need them tonight.

As she stepped closer, she realized she was already dry, except for her hair. The warm night air had quickly absorbed the moisture. She felt cool, refreshed.

"Tell, I don't want to jeopardize this job. It's very important to me."

"And seeing me would jeopardize it?" he asked.

"I don't know. Beverley was pretty specific."

"She may dictate what you do during working hours, but your free time's your own."

"Ordinarily, yes, but she's already said I shouldn't associate with you—what if she fires me?"

"Don't tell her." There was a thread of amusement in his

tone—and a hint of steel.

Molly hesitated, thinking what that would entail, wondering if she wanted to do that. She'd always been straightforward. To go behind Beverley's back and against her wishes seemed somehow dishonest.

Yet there was no denying her feelings. She was drawn to Tell Hardin. She liked being around him, though he overwhelmed her. Surely there'd be no harm in spending some of her free time with him? Just to see some of the sights of Acapulco. He'd offered.

She wouldn't neglect her work in any way.

And she knew better than to fall for him. He was charming and sexy and much too smooth and knowing for her to handle. But surely it couldn't do any harm to spend a few hours in his company.

And be the envy of all the women in town.

The thought sprang unbidden to mind. She smiled a little at that. She would be the envy of all who saw them. Tell was sexy as anyone she'd ever seen.

"Before you kick me to the curb, Molly, think of the fun we could have. I've been here before. I can show you the cliff-divers of La Quebrada, visit the underwater shrine of the Virgin of Guadalupe, go snorkeling, try the parachute rides or the moonlight cruises of the bay. We can bargain at the markets and ride horses on the beaches. What do you say?"

She smiled at the pictures his words painted. It sounded exciting, exotic... and expensive. She came back to reality with a bang.

"It sounds wonderful but very expensive. Just who's footing the bill for all this—me? Maybe that's what Beverley meant," she said evenly.

That would explain why a man as good-looking as Tell would spend time with her instead of picking up some of the more beautiful girls who filled the beaches.

"Now I've heard everything. What do you think, I'm some blasted gigolo?" He stood up abruptly and took a threatening step towards her.

"I don't know the first thing about you. You show up bringing towels. Why? To check out the new arrivals, see if burglary's an option. Or find one's an impressionable American girl to sweep off her feet with your charm and your good looks? Take her everywhere, but enjoy yourself, too, at her expense?"

"No one said you had to pay my way." His voice was hard, his stance taut, threatening.

"Oh, I suppose cowboys have lots and lots of money and camp out when they come to Acapulco just for the fun of it."

"What do you do, ask to see a man's bank balance before going out with him? If it meets your standards fine, if not, forget it? I wish you joy of your stay here."

He snatched up his clothes and stalked to the gate, vaulting over it to melt into the inky dark shadows of the hill. In seconds he disappeared without a sound.

"Tell."

Molly took a step towards the wall. She didn't want him to leave this way.

Even as she started after his departing figure, the knocker sounded on her door. Dinner had arrived. With a long look of regret at the dark hillside, she turned and quickly crossed the patio to her room.

She took the hibiscus from between her breasts, dropping it on the dresser as she passed. She shouldn't have been so outspoken. She didn't really think he was a gigolo, did she?

The question played over and over as she ate, showered and prepared for bed. Searching the empty patio one last time, she turned off her light and slipped beneath the sheet.

Tell hadn't returned. She hadn't expected him to–but she

wished that he had.

She shouldn't have said all that, but it was said partly from fear.

Fear she'd grow to like him too much, fear of what he'd demand from her. Life had been muddled and disruptive in her younger days and Molly fought for stability now. She liked things done in a proper and orderly fashion.

She couldn't afford to let some drifting cowboy turn her world upside down for a few weeks while he vacationed, then passed on. She just couldn't.

But had he already moved on?

The light from the sun was full on the patio when Molly awoke the next morning. She dressed in her new white shorts and a striped red and blue sleeveless top Tell had picked out. She wondered if he'd ever see her wear it. The top was short, exposing an inch of her midriff and she liked the feel of the warm, moist tropical air against her skin.

Her hair tied up off her neck, she wandered out to the patio. Spotting her glasses where she'd left them last night, she slipped them on and sank into the chair to eat the breakfast already laid out.

Beverley was not yet awake or at least had not opened her curtains. Molly felt free to enjoy the quiet morning air. The sun softly kissed her skin and she shifted her position to take full advantage of it. She wanted to get a tan quickly. Compared to the others on the beach yesterday, she'd looked positively pale.

Without conscious thought, she let her eyes scan the hillside. Where was Tell? Was his camp near by? He'd never said. Somehow she thought it closer to town, but then how did he get here? Their casita was one of the uppermost in the complex. There were only two higher than theirs. Terraced below them were dozens of casitas, each with its own patio, pool and spectacular view of Acapulco.

Breakfast finished, Molly was impatient to get started on her work. She found an electric outlet on the side of the casita and brought the computer out in the shade of the awning over the door. She had lots of work to do, but here she could glance up from time to time to see the bay and remembered how the sun had sparkled on from her vantage point on the beach.

She wished she and Tell had gone swimming at the beach.

Closing her eyes and leaning back in her chair she remembered Tell's face. Shifting her position, she retraced their time yesterday—in the shop yesterday, at the beach and the first night she'd met him. Last night when she'd insulted him and he'd left.

Opening her eyes, she was disgusted with herself for thinking so much about him. He was just a man she'd met a couple of times. Granted, the most exciting and sexy man she'd ever come across, but totally not for her.

Beverley kept a frantic pace for two days. Once she'd drawn open her curtains and slid her door open, she'd been hard to keep up with. She approved Molly's idea of moving the computer outdoors and except for the late afternoon when the sun was too worm, Molly loved transcribing all the tapes outside.

Beverly kept her recorder going day and evening, words pouring forth, ideas and scenes that had to be captured. Molly wondered whether she could keep up the pace for days on end.

Fingers flying, she improved her typing speed and was able to print out clean copy of the steady stream of words Beverley dictated each day.

Molly found herself growing more and more interested in the life and times of General Black Jack Pershing, the subject of Beverley's biography.

From time to time, however, mocking gray eyes danced before her. She'd lose track of Beverley's words and hear over and over the accusation Tell made.

It hurt that he never returned. Yet why would he, she had all but accused him of being a gigolo.

It was foolish, but each night she stayed out on the patio until late, hoping he'd come again and talk to her. She'd never been so caught up with another person before, so drawn to a man. She wanted to tell him of the work she was doing, hear what he was doing, hear about his life in Texas, share some of the sights of Acapulco as he had suggested.

Each night she sat alone on the patio. The beauty of the warm Mexican nights mocked her single status, The romance of old Mexico a fairy-tale to be dreamed of but not experienced.

She was lonely, a loneliness never before experienced. Was it the sweet scent of the evening air, the loveliness of the tropical night sky, or the beauty and romance that was Acapulco which emphasized her solitary state?

Or was it the memory of the few meetings she'd had with a romantic fantasy man. The way he'd made her feel so alive, so conscious of everything around her, from the beauty of the Mexican cosmopolitan city, to the loveliness of the blue waters and white sands of the bay?

So conscious of her own body and the emotions and longings he awakened within her. She wasn't sure whether she was glad she'd met him or annoyed she'd let him get under her skin as much as he had.

The next afternoon, Beverley stopped work at lunch.

"I want to lie in the sun, get some rays. I know it dries your skin, but, at my age, who cares?"

"I have one more tape to complete," Molly murmured as

she smiled up at the older woman.

"You can finish that up later. Run down to the gift shop for me. The kind of suntan lotion I like is sold there and I'm out. I want to put some on to help conserve what little moisture I have left. Also, see if they have any local fashion magazines. I always like to look at the fashions of the different countries when I visit. They can be so different from what we see in the States. Not that what we see in Los Angeles is representative of the whole US, mind you. The outlandish outfits I see on Rodeo Drive sometimes positively make me want to laugh out loud."

Her voice trailed off as she walked back to her room. Presumably to change, Molly thought, smiling as she attacked the last tape.

Beverley was easy to work for, made few demands and had plenty to say. Which is why she rarely stopped talking.

Reaching a stopping point, Molly was glad for the exercise walking down to the hotel gift shop would afford. She'd finish the last half of the tape later.

Since Las Casitas D'Oro was built on a hillside, the incline was steep. The roadway for the hotel was not wide so as she walked along the edge she kept a wary eye out for one of the hotel jeeps. Visitors to the hotel hurled around corners as if they owned the road and she didn't want to be hit by one.

The gift shop and lobby were together just inside the mighty stone pillars that marked the entrance. Passing the concierge desk, Molly paused, glancing at the man behind the ornate concierge desk. She slowed her pace as she thoughtfully entered the gift shop. Was that Miguel? Would he know where Tell was?

She looked for the items her employer had requested, charging them to their rooms. As she idly studied the other magazines, her heartbeat began to pick up as she considered talking to Miguel. Ask him about Tell.

Dare she? Would he know who she was, know of the last conversation she'd had with Tell? If Tell hadn't told him, Miguel might get a message to him.

Did he still know where to find Tell and how to reach him? Or had that been just for that one day? Was Tell within calling distance?

Heart pounding, stomach full of butterflies, Molly approached the desk. The young Mexican looked up and smiled at her, his eyes dark in his clean-shaven face.

"Excuse me, are you Miguel?" Molly asked.

"Si, senorita. How may I be of assistance to you?" The smooth rhythm of the Mexican accent was pleasant.

"I wondered if you know Tell Hardin? Know where I could reach him?"

"Senor Hardin is not staying at the hotel."

"I know. I just... one time he said I could leave a message with you to give to him. I wondered if I still could?"

"And the message?"

Molly stared at the man, her mind blank. What kind of message could she give? Come see me? After what she'd said? Her face fell. It was stupid to bother the concierge.

"I guess I don't have a message after all."

Dispiritedly, she turned away. How did you leave a message for a man whom you'd insulted? She was better off forgetting him. Only it was so much easier to say than to do.

Four

Knowing the angry accusations she'd made were the reasons Tell hadn't come around again, Molly had no one to blame but herself. How could she have blurted out such a thing? As she made the long climb back to their casita, she wished she could relive those few moments—she never would have said such a thing.

Joining Beverley on the patio, she handed her the sun screen. Leaving her for her swim, Molly went back to the computer to finish the last side of the tape.

Molly enjoyed the work. The information Beverley imparted was informative and entertaining. Though that lady talked a blue streak, her writing was succinct and enlightening. Molly wondered at the dichotomy.

Frowning, Molly also wondered how long it'd be before she stopped seeing Tell between her and the computer screen. Blinking her eyes only brought his image in better focus. She hadn't forgotten a single thing about him, from the way his skin crinkled slightly at his eyes when he smiled to the lips she'd longed to feel against hers.

She shook her head. She needed to finish the tape. She didn't want Beverley to find any fault with her work. This job was too important to her, the security it represented too precious to jeopardize by inattention.

When she finally finished, it was almost dinnertime. She sat back in her chair and gazed out over the pool, out beyond to the blue waters of the bay.

Only three nights ago she'd had an offer for dinner. She wished she had been able to take Tell up on his offer. Where would that have led them?

To the same angry words they'd sparred with on the patio? Or to different topics, different moods?

He'd asked her out and never said a word her paying.

Sighing, Molly closed her eyes. She should have had more information before accusing him. He'd suggested places to go, things to do and she'd immediately jumped to the conclusion he wanted her to treat. Why?

She knew it was because she couldn't believe an exciting man like Tell would want her company without something in return from her. She led a quiet life, struggling to make ends meet, no time for frivolous games. She knew so little about men in general and Tell specifically, aside from his pure animal magnetism.

How awful if she'd misjudged him.

Opening her eyes, she turned off the computer and called for room service. Another night alone in paradise.

Maybe she should change her clothes and go to one of the clubs in town. There'd be crowds of happy people, joyful music, and plenty of activity to entertain her.

She shrank away from the thought. She was too shy to venture forth on her own. And it wouldn't be as much fun with out Tell.

Darn it, was everything going to remind her of Tell Hardin? She'd only met the man a couple of times. Why had he made such an impression on her?

Molly had an early night, eager for the morning and the work that Beverley was sure to produce. She needed the fast-paced activity to take her mind off the turmoil of her thoughts.

To her surprise and disappointment, Beverley was not in the mood to write the next morning.

"I get like this sometimes," she said brightly, not at all deterred by her block. "I just pour myself into pages and pages, then can't do anything for a couple of days. I guess I have to recharge my batteries. I'll just lie in the sun or go shopping or call up some of my friends who live here. I'll be back on track either tomorrow or the next day. Don't worry about it. The only thing is, I never know when I'll be busy and when I won't. Take your free time now, because I might want to work non-stop for the next ten days."

"Isn't there something I can do to help?" Molly asked, thinking of research or editing. There must be something she could do to keep herself busy.

"No, nothing. I don't even want to think about it, though I'm probably thinking about it in my subconscious even as we speak. But that's not my conscious, so I don't know I'm thinking about it. But no, nothing now. It'll all come clear in another day or two. You go off and enjoy yourself."

Molly looked dismayed. Last night had been bad enough, long and endless and boring. What would she do with the whole day?

"Take the jeep. I'll call my friends. If I want to go anywhere, they can take me," Beverley said, pouring the last of the coffee into her cup.

"I really don't have any place to go," Molly said.

"Nonsense. If there's no place special you want to see, try the hotel's beach club. It has a couple of sheltered saltwater pools with tropical fish and plant life, or you can swim in the bay itself. They have a grand buffet there; you can have lunch and enjoy yourself. Don't give a thought to me. I'll be fine."

Beverley again reminded Molly of a bright, sprightly bird.

She hid her smile.

"Okay, maybe I'll try it."

Hanging around as long as she dared, to make sure Beverley didn't change her mind, Molly nevertheless started for the beach club by the late morning. She'd swim, eat lunch at the buffet and see what else there was to do. Maybe she'd venture into the city later, though she rather doubted she'd feel brave enough to go alone.

If all else failed, she'd brought a book.

She stopped in at the lobby, asking Miguel for directions to the beach club. Since Las Casitas D'Oro was situated high on a mountainside overlooking the bay, the drive to the beach was lengthy. She'd passed through some expensive residential sections of Acapulco before arriving at the private beach club belonging to the hotel.

Confident she knew where she was going once she received the directions, she started off slowly, still nervous in the open jeep.

Crossing the highway, she started down the hill. Tall palms and colorful pink and white oleander and red hibiscus lined the road. Behind stone walls she caught glimpses of the large villas built with their backs to the road, facing the view of the city, and the beautiful bay.

Stopping at one intersection, Molly was startled when a brown body came out of the shadows of the oleander and calmly slid into the seat next to her. His movements were smooth, like a sleek wolf on the prowl.

Molly's heart-rate increased as she recognized Tell Hardin. She became instantly aware of the brightness of the day, the rich tones of the red hibiscus and pink oleander lining the road. Despite the unfriendly words they'd exchanged, happiness welled within her at the sight of him.

"What are you doing here?" Not the most auspicious

greeting. She flushed and bit her lip. He'd never guess how glad she was to see him. She'd thought she'd never see him again.

He lifted his lips in a lazy smile and ran his eyes down her figure. She'd worn her bikini under the frilly, lacy cover-up. Her legs were beginning to tan and were shapely beneath the edge of the cover-up.

"You look good enough to eat," he drawled. "Where are you heading?"

She was flustered under his gaze and turned back to the road, easing across the intersection and starting down again.

"I'm going to the hotel's beach club," she told him primly.

"Nice place. We can go snorkeling there."

She threw him a dark glance. "It's for guests only," she said.

"You're a guest. I'm your guest. We're both guests."

She bit her lip in indecision. The dark thoughts from the previous night reared their heads. Did he want to spend time with her or was he using her only as a means to enjoy his holiday in places he wouldn't ordinarily afford?

She darted a swift glance, the indecision clearly written on her face. He didn't look as if he depended on a woman for anything.

"Tell, I don't think–"

"Good, don't. Did you miss me?"

Strong and rugged, he displayed an arrogant, don't- give-a-damn attitude that exuded confidence and assurance. The few times she'd been around him he'd taken charge, deftly, swiftly, totally. It didn't look as if today was any different.

She swallowed hard, not wanting to admit she'd missed him. Did nothing ever bother him?

"The truth now," he warned her, his tone full of amusement.

"Well, I did notice you weren't trespassing as much lately," she said, her eyes carefully on the narrow street.

He chuckled and drew a warm finger along her leg. Molly caught her breath, almost losing control of the jeep, almost losing control of herself. His touch was like an electric shock, sending delightful waves of pulsating pleasure through her.

"I thought your boss would be working you so hard you'd not even notice."

"I have today off," she said, achingly aware of his body just inches from her.

He was wearing cut-offs and scruffy sandals. Seeing his every move from the corner of her eye made it very difficult to concentrate on driving.

Her body was aware of his proximity, her leg craving further touches from his fingers. Her breathing became more laborious. She gripped the wheel, forcing her mind to concentrate on her driving.

"Good, we'll spend it at the beach club. They have a good lunch," he said.

"Tell—"

"Unless you're spending the day with someone else," he asked.

"No."

"Good. Here we are, turn here."

She came upon the gate sooner than expected and had to turn sharply to enter. The attendant smiled, recognizing the hotel's jeep, and waved her in. Molly couldn't believe how easy it was.

"Easy, if you know how," Tell murmured as she pulled into the parking area.

"I don't think you should be here."

She turned to him, not expecting the shock of desire that flooded when his eyes met hers.

She raised her gaze to clash with his and couldn't look away. His eyes were quizzical in the morning light, silvery gray and sparkling. Faint lines radiated from the corners, lighter in color than the rest of his skin. He must narrow his eyes against the sun. Did he look far distances when riding the range in Texas?

He reached up and withdrew her glasses. Molly blinked, but he was close enough to be in focus. She held her breath. What would come next?

"Do you have sunglasses?" he asked, his eyes dropping to her lips.

Molly licked them, her tongue flicking out quickly to wet them, withdrawing.

"Yes, in my tote."

"Put them on or you'll get wrinkles."

His gaze never left her lips and Molly dropped her own gaze to his mouth. Jerking her head away, she rummaged through her tote, finding the glasses and thankfully putting them on. They offered some measure of protection.

Tell smiled and climbed from the jeep, waited for her to come around and then headed for the water.

There were two large saltwater pools, separated from the bay itself by huge stone walls. Beneath each wall was access to the bay—the water in the pools constantly changed with the ebb and flow of the sea. Colorful chairs and recliners lined the deck of both pools, umbrellas here and there to shelter those wanting shade.

There was a motorized bar that circulated around on the wide paved areas and to the far side Molly saw the tables and buffet set for lunch beneath the shade of a blue and white awning. Tall palms swayed in the breeze, colorful flowers banked the hill as it rose from the bay. It was a beautiful setting.

"You didn't bring a towel," she said as she dropped her bag on one of the recliners.

"Don't need to; they provide them here."

"You've been here before, haven't you?"

He knew more about it than she did, and she'd read the brochure in the hotel room.

"Mmm, once or twice."

Who with? she wondered.

"Want to swim, snorkel, or lie in the sun?" Tell surveyed the area and nodded to the small booth with snorkel gear.

"I'd like to try snorkeling. I've never done it." Molly said, following his gaze.

He ignored what he didn't want to deal with. She wished she had that knack.

Tell walked casually over and spent several moments talking with the young man on duty there. He gathered up the masks, snorkels and fins and rejoined Molly.

She sat on one of the chairs, watching the transaction from a distance, feasting her eyes on the tall Texan who had invaded her life so suddenly and completely invaded her senses. Why had he singled her out for attention? He was almost too good to be true: rugged, handsome, confident.

That was the problem. He was too much to be taken by someone like her. What was his game?

Glancing around, she saw she wasn't the only woman watching Tell. Several others followed him with their eyes as he moved around the edge of the tidal pool. For a moment happiness threatened to overwhelm Molly—he was coming back to her. She was almost smug in her feelings. He hadn't glanced at any of the tanned beauties displaying themselves to best advantage in the morning sun.

He dropped the equipment on an adjacent chair when he reached her then pulled her to her feet. Before she could say anything, his hands moved to the ribbons holding her cover-up closed and slowly began to undo them. Drawing the moment out, he slowly pulled the first ribbon, the material falling open, then the second, and the third.

Tension rose in Molly until she could almost touch it. His eyes were intently watching the material fall open, watching as his fingers released the ribbons and slowly let the soft satin drift through his fingers before releasing it.

"You're always undressing me," she said softly.

Molly closed her eyes, mortified, not believing she'd said the words aloud. She felt the heat rise in her face. How could she blurt out something like that?

Remembering how she felt that evening by the pool, she knew she should demand he stop. But she didn't want to. She'd never felt so wanted, so feminine, so desirable in a man's eyes. For a moment, she didn't want to know the reason, she only wanted to enjoy the sensations as long as they lasted.

When she opened her eyes and ventured to look at Tell, he was gazing down at her, his eyes no longer amused or mocking, but serious.

"One day," he said softly, holding her gaze, "I won't stop at the swimsuit."

He waited a moment then the familiar amusement crept back into his eyes.

"Relax and enjoy yourself. Acapulco is for sun, sea, sand and sex."

Color stained her cheeks. Had she given him the wrong impression? Did he think she went in for casual sex?

Embarrassment flooded through her.

She had to set him straight, right now. She took a deep breath. She couldn't let him think–

Tell chuckled, his teeth white in the deep tan of his face. Taking her chin in his fingers, he tilted her face up a little.

"You aren't like anyone I know. I wish you could see the expressions chase across your face. Okay, if sex is out, we'll have fun other ways."

She frowned.

He was always laughing at her. Why did he spend time with her—because she gave him such great amusement?

She looked into his eyes and felt herself drowning in a silvery sea of emotions never experienced before.

She wanted him to kiss her and as the thought took hold it was all Molly could do to keep herself from throwing herself into his arms.

Her heart began beating heavily at the thought of having sex with Tell. It'd probably be wonderful. Great for her, but what about him?

She'd never know. She wanted more, want to make love, not just have the physical joining.

Wanted him to look on her as special, not just another girl picked up in Acapulco.

"Now what are you thinking?"

His voice was low, sexy, his thumb gently rubbing her chin, his eyes narrowed as he watched her.

"Nothing." Was that thready voice hers? She needed more resolution. She could so easily become devastated by this man—she had to resist.

Tell waited a moment to see if she'd say more, then he said, "Let's go snorkeling."

Tell helped her don the snorkels, face masks and fins and led Molly in the huge natural sea pool nearest their chairs. He showed her how to breathe, adjusted her flippers and dived cleanly into the water. Molly followed, knowing instantly she wasn't the swimmer he was.

But it didn't matter. He stayed right beside her while she marveled at the beauty beneath the surface of the water. The small tropical fish that darted before her outstretched hands were colorful, wearing patterns of yellow and blue and red. The light sand was a perfect background for the lacy seaweed that grew near the rocks, and the small pink and rose sea anemones that waved their arms in the gently moving water.

Molly was fascinated with the beauty of the setting and bubbling with happiness when Tell tapped her on her shoulder and motioned her upright.

She shook her head when she surfaced, drawing up the face mask, flipping some of her hair back. It was in the way—maybe she should cut it.

"It's wonderful." She smiled at him, her excitement evident in her face.

He smiled and nodded. "I know, but we have to stop now. Your back will be blistered if we don't. The water draws the sun and you're lying on top too much with your fair skin."

Knowing he made sense, she was still loath to stop. With one more reluctant look at the treasures beneath the surface, she slowly swam to the wall.

She wished she had the deep tan he had and wondered how he'd got so brown all over. Probably hanging out all summer long in Mexico, flirting with tourists, a new one every few weeks.

Tell was by the stone steps leading up to the patio, waiting for her. Trying to take off her flippers, Molly fell over, the water coming over her head, and she almost choked because of her laughter.

Despite all her gloomy thoughts, she was having a wonderful time with Tell Hardin. So what if it ended when she left Mexico, she'd enjoy every moment until then.

He hauled her up and held on to one hand, his laughter mingling with hers. She slipped off the flippers and reached up to take off the mask. The rubber strap was tangled in her hair.

"Ouch, I can't get it," she groaned.

"Turn around; I'll get it," he said.

She obediently turned in the chest-high water, swaying slightly in the movement of the gentle waves, her arms floating on the surface, lassitude and contentment spreading through her.

He pulled her hair a little and tears flooded her eyes.

"Ouch."

"Done." He turned her around, seeing the tears glimmer in the sun.

Molly saw the spiky lashes of his eyes coming closer, until she closed her own.

His lips touched hers, cool and salty.

Molly smiled and opened her eyes to see him draw back slightly. She felt as if she were dreaming, floating on a soft sea of emotions. She closed her eyes again and he kissed her again, but this time it wasn't a peaceful, dreamy kiss, it was fiery, electric, exhilarating. His lips were hot and demanding.

Her own moved in response as her body suddenly clamored for contact with him. She moved through the warm water up against his body, her arms encircling his neck and her lips moving feverishly against his. She sought to give whatever he demanded, moving to get closer, to feel the strength and warmth of his body against her own.

His hands moved down to caress the small of her back just above her bikini. His fingers trailed electric shocks of pleasure along her spine, across the sensitized muscles. She couldn't get close enough, moving her body against his as she tried to, her lips hot and responsive, moving against his, reveling in the feel of his mouth on hers, his hands bringing shimmering waves of delight, the strength of his chest, his legs.

He drew back, breathing heavily in the bright morning sun. Molly felt as if her only support was gone as she slowly let her hands drop from his shoulders, afraid to meet his look, self-consciousness weighing her down.

Could she just sink in the water and never come up again?

He tilted her chin once more and dropped a light kiss on

her lips.

"You should get your hair cut."

She blinked, not expecting that.

"Why?"

"First, it's got to be hot in this climate or in LA for that matter. Second, it wouldn't get tangled in snorkeling masks."

She stepped back, not knowing whether to be angry or not. After the magic of his kiss, all he thought about was her hair.

"But the real reason you should get it cut," he said softly, "is that it'd expose your pretty neck, the easier to reach."

Tell leaned over and kissed her softly on her neck, sweeping her damp tangled hair aside. Straightening, he smiled directly in her eyes.

Molly swallowed hard, her emotions on a roller- coaster. She was in over her head and didn't know what to do.

Five

Molly walked over in a daze to the lounger where her towel lay. She dried off and sat back, putting her sunglasses firmly in place. It gave her some shelter from Tell's penetrating gaze.

He followed her back and lay down in the lounger beside her, pulling the chair close to hers. The even rise and fall of his chest soon let her know he'd fallen asleep in the sultry air.

Molly lay still, though her mind raced. She'd finally been kissed, felt his firm lips moving against hers, knew what it was like to have his body against hers. But it was his lips that claimed her attention, hot and passionate. The feelings he evoked burned in her memory, through her body. Did he kiss everyone like that or only her? The tip of her tongue licked her top lip.

Her body suffused with heat as she relived those pulsating moments, she sat up, hoping for some cooling breeze to bring down her temperature. She might have to go back into the water or at the very least change the direction of her thoughts.

"What's wrong?" Tell asked lazily from beside her.

She looked over. He hadn't even opened his eyes. How did he know anything was wrong?

"I'm hot," she said, holding her breath, hoping he wouldn't ask why.

"I know, it's hot as blazes out here. Hold on, I'll get us an umbrella."

His supple body rose effortlessly from the recliner and he crossed easily across the hot cement. In only seconds he returned with a large umbrella that shaded both their chairs. Setting it up, he moved his chair closer to Molly's and sank back down, eyes closing.

"Thank you," she murmured, turning slightly so she could watch him.

His lips turned up slightly, but he didn't open his eyes.

"Tell me what you've been doing since I saw you last," he ordered.

Molly launched into an account of the work she'd been doing for Beverley, the long hours, how interesting it all was for her, keeping a wary eye on him, in case he grew bored.

"She's quite different from what I expected, but she's fascinating to work for."

"You haven't worked for her for long?"

"No, I just got the job before we came here. My old job ended and I thought I'd be out of work for a while, but I found this right away. It pays well and there's the extra bonus of travel. I never thought I'd see Acapulco."

"Nice perk. Tell me about LA."

Molly sank back, closing her eyes, slowly telling Tell some of what her life was like, glossing over how alone and lonely she was.

Briefly she mentioned that her parents were dead, but didn't tell him of the struggle it'd been to make ends meet when her mom had been alive. She didn't talk of how lacking basic security as a child after her father deserted them made her value security above all else.

Instead she emphasized her progress in work, the reading and sewing she liked to do for relaxation.

Then she paused, not wanting to talk about herself—she knew about that. She wanted to learn more about Tell.

"What about you? What's it like being a cowboy?" she asked.

"I like it. Riding most days, fooling with stupid cattle. But the range is open and free and I can do what I want, when I want. I don't have to answer to anyone. I'm outside all the time, which I like. Though not so much in the rain."

She could picture him on a tall horse, sitting proud in the saddle, and looking over the miles of open range that stretched out before him.

She tried to imagine him in an office, or shop, but was unable to do so— he belonged to the outdoors.

"Want lunch? The buffet's good," Tell said.

Molly opened her eyes, a vague sense of unease troubling her. How did he know so much about this place?

"Sure."

She donned her frilly white cover-up and they strolled over to the tables set up under the colorful awning. There was a slight breeze and with the shade from the sun it was.

The buffet table was long, with all sorts of salads and cold meats and cheeses and tall fruit punches and glasses of iced tea.

Molly loaded her plate with the tropical fruit salads, wanting to eat the mangoes and passion fruit not readily found in the US. She was passing another offering, when Tell stopped her.

"Take some ceviche. You've never tried it, I bet."

"No, what is it?"

"Take some and try it. It's a local specialty, I'll bet you love it."

He scooped a portion on to her plate and a more generous one on his own.

Taking a glass of iced tea, Molly found a table near the water. A mariachi band played softly in the background. She

62

surveyed the view, the sparkling blue water, tall, stately palms swaying in the breeze, the cloudless sky, the circle of hills that enclosed Acapulco Bay.

And the tall, dark man coming to sit across from her.

Molly felt daring and reckless and slightly improper.

Lunch turned out to be more fun than she expected. Tell told her stories of Texas and experiences he'd had in his work with an amusing, mocking inflection. She laughed at his tales, knowing they had to be exaggerated, but finding them entertaining and enlightening.

When he asked her questions, she glossed over things, giving away little about herself. She didn't have a happy childhood to remember and didn't want the dark memories she did have spoiling her happy day.

And it was happy. She felt daring and free and all because of the way he looked at her, the way he spoke of things designed to make her laugh.

Yet his eyes spoke of other things, which made her breathless at times, very aware of the man opposite her.

After they'd eaten, Molly was presented with the bill. She looked up into Tell's eyes, startled into remembering her accusation of the other evening. Dropping her eyes before his steely glint, she knew he remembered as well.

She signed the ticket, writing her room number down. She'd have to settle with Beverley later for Tell's lunch. Molly didn't expect her boss to foot that bill.

She wondered how she would explain it to her boss.

But some of the sparkle of the day dimmed for her. Was he only here for what he could get from her? To further enjoy his vacation at her expense? What if she hadn't let him come to the beach club—would he have wanted to take her somewhere else?

When she rose, he slipped beside her, his hand encircling her upper arm, his fingers gripping hard. Quickly he half marched her from the dining area, out into the brilliant, hot sunshine. Passing their chairs, he continued around the point of land, around the banks of oleander to the side facing the Pacific Ocean. There was no one else on this stretch of beach; the wind was stronger and the surf powerful.

"I'm not some damned gigolo, Miss Gold-digger. If it's so important to you, I'll bring you the money enough for lunch tonight."

He jerked her in front of him, glaring down at her through narrowed slate-gray eyes.

She was frightened—his anger was so intense. She knew he had no money on him. His shorts and swimsuit were too revealing to permit even a folded peso in the pockets. Anyway, one meal among friends was nothing. If he continued to cadge off her, she could always say no if she thought he was taking advantage of her.

But she didn't want him angry.

"I don't want any money. I was enjoying the day, Tell. I'm glad you came with me." Her voice was soft. She raised her eyes as high as his lips, they started to soften and she dared a glance up.

His head blotted out the sky and his mouth found hers in a compelling kiss. His lips were hot demanding a response Molly was only too eager to give. His hand slipped beneath her cover-up and pulled her to his hard, warm body. His legs spread to hold them both and the kiss deepened as he moved urgently against her mouth, opening her lips and plunging deep within the hot moisture.

Molly's world exploded with sensation and quivered with passion. Her legs threatened to fail her, her arms found themselves around his neck, holding on, pulling him close. She couldn't think, only feel, feel the wondrous excitement building at his touch. The blood pounded in her head, blotting out the muffled roar of the surf behind her. Her heart raced, her breathing stopped.

Tell moved to trail fiery kisses along her cheek, nip her earlobe, move down her throat, kissing the fluttering pulse at its base. Molly closed her eyes, caught up in the physical delight of his touch. She never wanted the moment to end. Her skin on fire for his touch, and the touch of his hands only intensified the delight.

Sanity said, it had to end. They were on a public beach, where anyone could wander by at any time. Reluctantly, she opened her eyes, dazzled in the bright sunlight, her nerve-endings quivering in aroused passion, longing for more, much more. She was shocked at her own response to him.

"Tell," she said softly, imprinting the feel of his hot lips on her throat for all time, memorizing the feel of his muscles beneath her fingers, the strength of his shoulders and the tantalizing feel of the crisp hair on his strong chest.

These she would always remember. Her fingers were reluctant to leave, she was reluctant to stop, but they must.

"Tell, please, we need to stop."

"Why?"

He looked down at her eyes, his like molten steel, smoldering and passion-drugged. Flicking to her mouth and back to her eyes, he asked again, "Why, Molly, don't you like it?"

"Yes. I do."

She struggled to stand away from him, before she lost all sense of decorum. "Too much. Tell, we're on a public beach."

He smiled at her, the passion gradually fading to be replaced with the familiar amusement. "And that's a problem because why?"

"Well, I think we should—"

"What we should do is go back to my camp where there's

no one around for miles and make long, slow, passionate love. While the afternoon away and sleep together tonight."

Color stained her cheeks and she pushed against his shoulders.

"I can't do that," she whispered.

What would her employer say? She couldn't jeopardize her job.

He let her slip back. "No, I don't think you could."

He sighed. Stupid of him. One of the things that appealed to him about Molly Spencer was her naivety, her innocence. He'd never met anyone like her and he wanted to get to know her better.

But pushing her to become like other women he knew wasn't the way to find out what made her special. That'd be forcing her into the same mold as all the others.

What was it about her that had him coming all protective around her? He was here for R&R, not to pressure some innocent into an affair that'd cross all her boundaries and cause more harm then happiness.

Though he had no doubts she'd make him happy if she came back to his tent. And he knew he'd take her to heaven whenever she was ready.

He wondered if that could ever be prior to his leaving for home.

Molly looked over his left shoulder, across the white sands of the beach. Because of the heavy surf, it wasn't used by the sun-and-sea-loving crowd. But someone could venture along the beach for a walk.

"Come on, there's some hammocks over there. We can check them out and then go swimming later."

Tell slowly let his hands slide down her body, slip out from beneath her frilly cover-up. He wanted to pull her down on the sand and make love all afternoon. Instead, they'd lie in the hammocks and let a glorious opportunity pass.

Taking one of her hands in his, he started across the sand to the large hammocks spread beneath a thatched awning. Sheltered from the hot sun, open to the breeze and the view of the Pacific, it was an ideal spot for a nap.

If anyone could sleep.

Tell sat on the edge of one, Molly right in front of him. Leaning back, Tell brought her down on top of him, gazing into her eyes with smoldering passion.

Laughter filtered to them. Looking up in startled awareness, Molly saw a group of five or six people round the headland and start towards the beach. Struggling, she moved to get up, to have Tell release her.

He sat up and glaring at the newcomers. They were too far away to see his expression and gaily waved.

He lay back on the hammock and reached for Molly, pulling her down beside him.

"I guess the fun's over for now. We'll relax and wait until they leave."

Relax? Molly had no chance to relax next to Tell. Her body temperature rose to rival that of the sun. Every cell in her body yearned for his touch. She wanted kisses and caresses and more.

Yet to put any distance between them endangered their precarious balance on the hammock. She closed her eyes, determined to regain her composure, determined to regain control of her emotions and senses before she did something utterly foolish, like love him right out in front of everyone.

Slowly as he made no move except to push the hammock slightly so they swayed in the breeze, Molly began to relax. Before long, she dozed off.

The sun was low on the horizon when Molly awoke. She was sprawled across Tell, her head resting on his chest, one arm thrown over him. Blinking, she sat up to stare down at his familiar mocking smile.

"You're supposed to fall asleep after sex, not before it," he murmured.

Realization flooded through her and she scrambled off the hammock, tipping it over and dumping Tell on the sand. She started towards the pool area at a fast walk.

"Molly."

She wasn't one to go in for casual vacation affairs, nor was she so confident of her future that she'd tie her life to an indigent cowboy without two cents to his name.

Even if he asked her to, which he never had.

"Wait." His exasperated voice sounded behind her.

Molly quickened her pace.

She reached her things before Tell caught up with her.

She was surprised, but didn't stop to wonder what he was doing. She didn't care. She just wanted to get away heart-whole and fancy free. She had no business mixing with that dangerous Texas cowboy.

When she reached the jeep, there was still no sign of him. For a moment she was surprised. With his longer legs he should have overtaken her by now.

No matter—he'd wanted to come to the beach club and he had. Now let him find his own way back.

She slammed the jeep in gear and took off, driving as all the other jeep drivers did, wild, reckless and fast.

Molly half expected Tell to come to the patio that night so she stayed in her room with the air- conditioner on and the curtains closed.

Though she peeked out from time to time, she didn't see him.

She refused to be disappointed, though the ache in her

heart was very close to disappointment.

She was in Mexico to work, not to spend time with some fun-loving cowboy.

Beverley still wasn't in the mood to write the next morning, so Molly decided to venture forth into Acapulco on her own. She knew she could find the same parking garage they'd used before. She'd explore the city from that point.

Since the Avenida Costera Miguel Almeda hugged the beach from one end to the other, she had only to head for the water to find her way around.

Wearing a pair of navy shorts and a pink cotton sleeveless top, she took a deep breath. The sultry heat of the city streets was stifling. Tying her hair up out of the way, she gave a thought to having it cut. It'd definitely be more convenient in this climate and Beverley had intimated that they'd be staying several weeks.

But if she'd got it cut, Tell would think she cut her hair to suit him.

Window shopping and gazing at the fabulous displays that lined the busy thoroughfare was fun. She enjoyed the festive feel of the town.

At one of the large hotels along the avenue, she paused a moment then went inside.

An hour later she was again walking down the street, her hair in short curls, her head lighter, her neck cooler. She paused before a small mirror, smiling at the sight. Was that her? She took off her sunglasses to see better. The curls danced in the afternoon breeze, the tan she'd acquired since arriving gave becoming color to her face, her blue eyes seemed deeper than ever. She looked almost pretty.

Involuntarily, she smiled.

She walked along, smiling at her pleasure in her new look. A man walking towards her smiled broadly in return, winked at her and paused a moment as she walked by, staring unabashedly at her.

Molly's spirits rose.

She found her way to the Zocalo, the heart of Acapulco. There were rows and rows of stalls in the open air market, selling everything from brightly colored cloth to straw hats, brass ware, carved wooden figures and pretty jewelry.

The square was crowded as tourists vied with each other while trying to find the best bargains they could. The bustling activity intrigued Molly and she paused, stepping to the side, to watch the action.

When she grew tired of people watching, she looked back towards the main street. Her eyes widened. Across the aisle, coming from one of the open stalls, was Tell. He was limping. Her puzzled look dropped to his feet; one was wrapped in a white bandage, dirty on the edge by his flip-flops.

"Tell," she called, moving towards him.

He looked around at the sound of her voice, but didn't recognize her until she was close. His eyes widened when he saw her, his mouth splitting into a big grin. Briefly his gaze flicked down the length of her and Molly was instantly aware that the clothes she wore had been chosen by this man.

"Well, aren't you the pretty one, darlin'?" he said, studying the effect of the shorter hair.

She blushed with happiness at his compliment, flushing slightly when she recalled his reasons she should get her hair cut.

"I didn't get it cut because of you," she said quickly.

"Of course not." His amusement told her he didn't believe her.

He limped over to stand beside her, his eyes dancing in the sunlight. Audaciously he leaned over and placed a warm kiss on her neck.

"Tell, what happened to your foot?"

Her hand reached out and touched his arm, unable to keep away. His skin was warm, the muscles taut.

He shrugged. "When you ran off so abruptly, I followed and cut my foot on some jagged shells. Required two stitches. I'm supposed to be on vacation, not sitting in a hospital."

"Oh, Tell, I'm sorry."

He shrugged. "It's not that big a deal. I've been hurt worse on the ranch. Why did you leave so fast?" His eyes bore down into hers.

"I... things... it was getting..." She floundered. How to explain why she left? She wasn't sure herself.

"I told you there'd be no sex if you didn't want it. I've never forced myself on a woman yet and I wouldn't start with you."

"I didn't think you would," she said miserably. But at the time she hadn't been so sure. Or had it been her own ability to say no that she doubted?

"If it's the money—" He reached into his pocket.

"No, it's not the money. Honestly, I just had to leave. I'm sorry you got hurt."

"Getting the sand cleaned out wasn't a picnic and I can't go in the water for a few days, but otherwise it isn't a big deal. What are you doing in town? Is your boss near by?"

He looked around the busy marketplace, teeming with all nationalities.

Beverley was so short that she'd be swallowed up in a crowd like this one.

"She's visiting friends again today. I have the day off."

Tell's face closed up and he seemed to withdraw. Molly felt hurt. Yesterday when she'd told him that she had the day free he'd wanted to spend it with her. Today, he didn't seem to want to be around her at all.

Not that she could blame him—if she hadn't left so

abruptly they'd have parted friends. He would have watched where he was going instead of chasing after her and cutting his foot. She glanced at his foot, wishing she could turn back the clock.

"Shopping, I guess," he said.

"I wanted to go sightseeing a little, too. I don't know when I'll have another day off, and I thought I could see some of the sights today."

She stared at him hopefully, willing him to ask her to spend the day with him. Longing for his company.

"It's a nice day for it, though it will get hotter later. Enjoy."

He turned and began to limp down the main street.

Molly watched him leave in dismay. She counted on his wanting to spend time with her. Had he other things planned for today?

"Tell." She hurried after him. "Tell."

He paused and waited for her to catch up, his eyes drifting over her brief outfit. Molly felt suddenly conscious of how much skin showed.

"Would you like to go with me?" she asked hopefully, breathlessly.

"After you examine my bank account to make sure I'm acceptable, darlin'?" he asked, his eyes narrowed, flinty in color.

Molly realized she could know how he felt by the color of his eyes—he was angry again.

She flushed with shame, knowing her accusation that he was a gigolo burned.

"My treat," she said softly. "Please."

"No, not your treat. If I go with you, it'll be Dutch all the way. I'll pay my own way, you pay yours, exhibits, purchases or food. Agreed?"

She nodded eagerly at his terms. She'd agree to almost anything to spend a few more hours in his company.

"First thing, then, the calandrias."

He placed his hand on the small of her back, guiding her across the pavement and towards one of the gaily decorated horse-drawn carriages lined up at the curb.

Molly smiled in secret amusement. He'd taken over in less than two seconds. What if she had other plans?

Not that she did.

She was glad he agreed to go with her, however, and would gladly go wherever he suggested. He knew the best places to see, the sights not to miss. She'd let him take charge–not that she apparently had much choice.

She was enchanted with the carriage, which was shiny and polished, decorated with ribbons and bright balloons. The black horse pawed on the ground as if letting her know he was as anxious as she was to start. Tell handed her up into the open carriage and spoke rapidly in Spanish to the driver. Climbing in after Molly, he sat back beside her.

"A tour of the city. Best way to see it first," he murmured, looking out as the horse began his walk head tossing.

He seemed more interested in pointing out the sights of Acapulco than in her, but Molly herself was soon caught up in the tour. She eagerly looked where directed by the driver or Tell, captivated by the contrasting places of the old Mexican city as Tell translated everything the driver said. From the glittering high-rise resort hotels to the secrets of old town, she was fascinated. The shops and market stalls and open-air restaurants vied with the street hawkers selling everything from silver to pretzels. Old-fashioned horse drawn carriages and sleek sports cars of all types jammed the main street.

They stopped at La Quebrada, where the cliff divers plunged over one hundred and forty feet into the sea in a narrow, rocky gorge, timing their dives with the surging water.

A miscalculation and the diver could end up dead.

Sipping an iced juice on the veranda of La Mirador, Molly watched with fascination as a young man accomplished his daring feat. A few minutes later he was walking among the observers, seeking tips. Beaming when he approached her, she gave him a bill. Darting a quick glance at Tell, she saw him give a like amount.

"Dutch all the way," he murmured, catching her eye as he cocked an eyebrow her way. His gaze held hers for a long moment.

Molly looked away, not sure how to respond. There were none of the overtures he'd given yesterday. They could be total strangers for all the attention he paid to her.

Molly was piqued. Yesterday he'd been pushing her, kissing her, urging her to make love to him. Why was he so stand-offish today? She flushed when she realized where her thoughts were going.

The reason she'd left so abruptly yesterday was that she'd been scared. Had a day made a difference? Did she want him to kiss her?

The calandria took them to the Plaza Juan Alvarez, at the other end of the old town, to see the Acapulco cathedral. It appeared both unusual and exotic to Molly with its Byzantine towers and mosque-like dome. Beautiful and ornate, it dominated the Plaza.

El Fuerte De San Diego was the most historic place in Acapulco, a fort built to defend the town when it was a sea port connecting Mexico with the Orient. The walls had stood for centuries. She could imagine the Spanish soldiers who had guarded the city so far from their home. Had they grown to love this foreign land to enjoy it's location by the sea? Or had they always pined for the refined Spanish life they'd left behind?

Molly began to grow tired, but didn't want to let Tell know. It would shorten their time together.

She glanced at the usually clear blue sky. It was clouding over. Were they due for rain? She'd heard of the quick showers that soaked the area for a few hours and then stopped. The sky was darkening.

Afraid he'd say goodbye when the tour was over, Molly tried to think of something she could say or do that'd let him know she didn't want their time to end when they finished the tour. She didn't know why he remained so aloof today. If she had a clue, perhaps she could recapture the earlier friendliness.

He hadn't even laughed at her today. She didn't realize how much she relished his teasing until he stopped.

They were almost back at the starting-point and she still hadn't come up with anything to say that would keep him around.

"I've enjoyed seeing the city," she said, frowning when she heard how prim she sounded. Still it'd done some good–he looked at her with some of the amusement he normally displayed.

She rushed into speech before he could speak. "I mean, it was better than going by myself. No, that sounds wrong. Okay, I liked seeing it with you."

"Glad you enjoyed it."

Now he sounded almost too polite. Not at all like the brash Texan she was used to fighting off.

"Is your foot hurting?" she asked.

"A bit. I guess walking around on it wasn't the best thing to do today. I think I'll call it quits and head for camp."

"Want a ride? I have the jeep."

He climbed down from the carriage and spoke at length with the driver, giving him a large handful of bills. Molly jumped down and went to stand by him, opening her purse.

"How much is my share?" For a moment she thought he wasn't going to answer her.

"About twelve dollars US."

She did sums in her head and fished out the foreign currency, carefully counting it out in his hand. Snapping her purse closed, she looked up.

"Do you want a ride to camp? I could help you with dinner."

There, if he didn't want her around he could say so.

She held her breath, afraid he'd do that very thing.

His eyes crinkled in amusement and he smiled for the first time that afternoon.

"Sure, that I'd like to see. Where's your jeep?"

Happiness bubbled up inside as Molly led the way to the garage. Her time with him wasn't over yet. And she'd see where he was staying and share the evening meal with him.

She refused to think beyond that, afraid of where her thoughts might lead. For now it was enough that she was spending some more time with Tell Hardin.

Six

As they walked to the car park, Molly noticed that the afternoon breeze seemed stronger and cooler than earlier. She darted a quick glance at the darkening sky. It looked as if it might pour down rain at any time. She debated saying something to Tell, afraid he'd change his mind about letting her come to his camp if he thought it was threatening rain.

She was exceedingly curious about where he was staying. If he didn't notice the impending rain, she'd not be the one to tell him.

A wolf-whistle broke into Molly's concentration and she looked up, startled to see a young Mexican grinning at her. She smiled shyly back, flattered. She'd never had someone whistle at her before.

Tell's hand came out to grasp hers and she looked at him in surprise.

"Cutting your hair was a big mistake, I can see that," he said, glaring at the young man. "Everyone in Acapulco will be after you now."

Molly was aglow from his compliment, her heart swelling with delight. She didn't believe him, but was elated that Tell had said it.

"I doubt that," she murmured, tightening her fingers around his hand, feeling the tough skin of his palm and fingers against the softness of her own. Her arm tingled with his touch and she was suddenly assailed with doubt.

He'd wanted her to come to his camp yesterday, where he'd wanted to make long, slow, passionate love to her. What was he expecting now?

She threw him a glance. Did he think she'd changed her mind now that she agreed to go with him? She hesitated a step. Maybe she shouldn't go.

Before she could think of a reasonable excuse, they were in the jeep and heading out of town. As she followed Tell's directions to his camp, she wondered how he got around the way he did. He was miles from town. They followed one of the mountain roads leading up from the beach area, climbing higher and higher until they were far from the populated neighborhoods of Acapulco, the area spread behind them like a relief map.

Stopping at a large wooden gate, Tell hopped down from the jeep and swung the gate open. When Molly passed through, he closed it and climbed back into the jeep.

"How do you get to town or to Las Casitas D"Oro?" she asked, turning on to the dirt-road where he directed.

"I rented a car."

"Where is it now?"

"In town."

She was silent while she processed that. He had his own transport, he hadn't needed hers. She smiled quietly. Her conclusion—he wanted to spend time with her as much as she wanted to be with him.

"So after dinner, when you have to go home, you'll have to give me a ride back into town to fetch it," he murmured, his eyes on her.

She nodded, suddenly afraid to face him. She was conscious of how near he sat, how alone they were in the pretty little valley that opened up before them. To the east the taller mountains of the Sierra Madre rose, and yet the ridge to the west blotted out all views of Acapulco and the sea. They were in their own little world.

She saw the small tent, in a grassy meadow. He motioned her to park near by and she pulled in right where he indicated.

Molly noticed Tell's limp again as he led the short distance to his camp and guilt struck her. She hadn't needed to panic yesterday and run off the way she'd done–he hadn't threatened her. She'd acted like an idiot, running scared. But it wasn't Tell she was afraid of.

She'd try to make it up to him. She could cook dinner, at least.

But Tell wouldn't let her do a thing. He had her sit on a small log near the fire he built and talked to her as he worked quickly and efficiently.

She watched, fascinated, as he started a stew for dinner in a big cast iron pot. He even baked a small apple crumb cake for dessert in an iron skillet. He made it look so easy. She'd never have managed so well.

The meal was delicious.

Tell kept her entertained with stories of his childhood in south Texas along the Rio Grande. Growing up with cows and horses and riding to school until he reached high school, when trucks and cars held more appeal than horses.

"So there were five of you," Molly said at one point, trying to keep all the brothers and sisters straight.

"In my immediate family, but I have dozens of cousins. And aunts and uncles and grandparents— everyone's always dropping by, so it's hard to tell who lives there and who doesn't sometimes."

"What do your brothers and sisters do now?" she asked as she finished the last of her cake. She wished there was more.

The coffee was delicious and she settled back to sip that while Tell told her more.

"One brother's a–ah–cowboy, like me. The other's in the Air Force. One sister's a lawyer, the other's a homemaker, with three kids already. I don't think they're stopping at that, either."

"Are they all married?"

"No, just the Captain, and Diane."

"And where are you?"

"Here."

"No," she giggled softly, smiling up into his eyes. "I mean, where in birth order, oldest?"

"Yep. How about you?"

Molly's smile faded. She didn't have fun stories to tell of her childhood, nor of any part of her life. She had to work too hard to keep going.

"I'm an only. An orphan, as a matter of fact. My folks died when I was young." She sipped her coffee, her eyes on the fire.

"And?" he prompted.

"I was sent to live with distant relatives, but that didn't work out, so then it was foster homes."

"That's tough." His voice was soft, sympathetic.

She refused to look at him or feel sorry for herself. She had only herself to depend upon and she was working hard for enough security to satisfy her in an insecure world.

"If you did things right, you got to stay?" he hazarded a guess, and Molly looked up, startled. How had he known?

She nodded slowly.

"I can't imagine anyone not wanting you to stay with them," he said, holding her eyes with his own. "If you had to move from family to family, it wasn't because you were bad or did something wrong—probably economics."

"Maybe. Anyway, security's very important to me. I need to know I won't end up like my mother, destitute and with a kid to support."

Without warning a gust of wind blew across the field, a torrent of cold rain immediately following. Molly hadn't given a thought to the threat of rain since she'd arrived.

The sky was dark, and looked as if the storm had been building for some time, but she and Tell had been caught up in their conversation, not paying attention to the weather.

Gasping in the shock of the deluge, Molly scrambled up, looking wildly for shelter. They were some yards from the tent, further from the jeep which had no top. Tell grabbed her hand and hurried over to the small tent, running as fast as his injured foot would allow. Molly couldn't see three yards in front of her; the rain was pouring down, cold and wet. The wind blew it every which way.

In only seconds she was soaked to the skin, her short hair dripping in her face, her legs streaked with water and splattered with mud.

They huddled just inside the opening, looking over at the fire, which was being extinguished by the deluge. Twilight was fading fast, hastened no doubt by the storm.

Molly shivered. She was soaked. It didn't feel much like the hot tropics right now.

"Boy, that was quick. I noticed earlier that it looked as if it might storm, but forgot about it while we were talking. I have some towels—wait while I find them. And get a light," Tell said, moving toward the back of the tent.

Molly couldn't see him in the dark, couldn't see anything in the tent, the light from outside too faint. But she heard him rummaging through his things. A strong flashlight suddenly illuminated their shelter and she saw Tell offer her a fluffy yellow towel.

Molly dried her dripping hair and mopped up the water from her arms and legs. Her skimpy top clung to her like a second skin, clammy and cold. Her shorts were soaked, too. She shivered slightly in the damp air, the temperature already dropping.

"How long do you think it'll last?" she asked, wiping the rain from her glasses, laying them near the opening, out of the way. Should she try to drive home now? She couldn't get any wetter.

"Don't know—an hour or two. It'll blow over before midnight."

"I'm cold."

"Me, too. Wet clothes do that. The temperature'll drop even more with the rain. We can change into dry things—it'll help. If you're still cold after that, well, I know something to warm you up."

Molly stared at him in the faint illumination, heat rising in her cheeks. She knew what he was saying, but refused to rise to the bait.

"I don't have any other clothes," she said, ignoring the hint he threw out.

"I have something you can wear." Tell threw her a blue denim work shirt, long-sleeved. "Try that."

Molly knelt in the dirt and stared at him. The tent wasn't more than seven feet long nor more than four or five feet wide. Just where was she to change into this shirt?

Tell drew off his shirt and tossed it into a sodden heap near the opening, pulling on a sweatshirt. When he raised his hips and unzipped his cut-offs, Molly turned and looked out on the rainy landscape, shivering a little. She was cold.

"Quite a dilemma, isn't it?"

The mocking tone was back. Molly thought she hated him at that moment.

Resolutely, she shook out his shirt and laid it across her knees. With her back to him, she drew her pink top over her head and tossed it to join his shirt. She unfastened her wet bra, and it followed suit. She quickly drew on his shirt and buttoned it up in front, to the collar. She raised herself on her knees and unfastened her shorts. Her panties were of nylon and would dry in minutes. These she left on, easing the shorts down and off. Refusing to turn around to face Tell, she slowly rolled up the huge sleeves so that her hands could be free.

Would he try to make love to her?

Her blood surged through her veins at the thought. He didn't need to for her to warm up, the mere thought of it accomplished that.

"Are you still cold, darlin'?" his soft voice asked in her left ear, as his hands took hold of her shoulders and his lips left fiery kisses on her neck.

She nodded, afraid to speak. Gently, he pulled her back against him, until she was resting against his warm chest, his jeans clad legs on either side of hers. His arms came around and crossed over her, just beneath her breasts, as he enveloped her in his warmth. Resting his chin on her shoulder, he held her and they looked out through the opening at the rain on the field.

Molly remained still, savoring the feel of his body against hers, his arms enclosing her. His body heat dispelled the chill from the rain. She could sit this way forever. It was heavenly.

"How will I get home?" she asked after several minutes of silence, except for the rain pounding on the tent.

"When it's blown over, we'll dry off the seats in the jeep and be ready to go. I'll need to get my car."

She stirred and pulled away, afraid to remain in such proximity any longer. Her thoughts were no longer about going home and that was dangerous.

"So what do we do until then?"

The rain was coming down as strongly as ever. Would it really end within a few hours?

"You can tell me more about you and I can tell you more about me. But we can be more comfortable if we sit on the sleeping-bag. This dirt is hard."

Tell moved away and Molly watched him pulling things from the back. He spread open his sleeping-bag, tossed his duffel bag to one side. The soft glow of the powerful flashlight gave the illusion of warmth in the tent.

Tell sprawled out on the sleeping-bag, lying on one elbow and watched Molly. His lips turned up slightly as he took in her appearance. The denim shirt fit her like a short dress that was much too big for her. Her hair was still damp but beginning to curl and she was kneeling, sitting back on her heels.

"The shirt looks better on you than me," he said, his eyes a silvery gray. "But you look like a nun with it buttoned to the top. Unfasten a couple of buttons." His voice was low, sexy, seductive.

Molly stared at him, fascinated by the look in his eyes, the smoky, smoldering stare he gave her as he waited for her to obey his command. She licked her lips, her heart beginning to beat rapidly. With nerveless fingers, she raised her hand and slowly slipped the first button through the hole. She couldn't look away.

Tell's eyes never left hers as they narrowed in assessment. "Do another," he said softly, daring her.

Was she hypnotized that she couldn't look away, couldn't function on her own? Slowly she slid the second button through the material. The heat pulsating through her body warmed her, making her intensely aware of the man lying carelessly across his sleeping-bag only a few feet away. Her eyes couldn't leave his; they were compelling, irresistible, seductive.

"Another."

She took a shaky breath and slid another through the material, wondering if he would have her open the entire front of the shirt.

Molly was conscious of the cotton material touching her, enfolding her, caressing her. It had last touched Tell's shoulders and chest; now it warmed her own skin. She felt a peculiar delight spread throughout her body. Dared she moved to join him on the sleeping- bag? The ground was hard, but she was afraid to move.

The material separated slightly, the skin exposed hinting at curves in the shadows.

With almost a groan, Tell sat up and reached out for her, drawing her to him on the sleeping-bag. He wrapped his arms around her and pulled her against his chest. Molly resisted for only a moment, then lay compliant against him. She loved the strength of the man, the excitement and daring she felt around him.

Tell lay back, pulling part of the sleeping-bag over Molly to keep the chilled air from her bare legs.

"Okay?" he asked, stroking her damp hair.

She could scarcely breathe, much less talk. Every inch of her skin was attuned to Tell, longing for him to touch her, longing for the feel of his skin against hers, his mouth against hers.

"No." She struggled away from him, pulling back and scooting across the opened sleeping-bag.

Eyes wide, she stared back at a startled Tell. How could she tell him she just couldn't allow herself to become taken with a drifting cowboy? She'd had a hard life and she didn't want to make any mistakes that'd perpetuate that. If she became intimate with a man, it would be with someone who was established, who could provide her with the basics of security.

"Now what?" His tone was exasperated.

"I... nothing. I... if we are going to talk, we can talk. I'm warm now," she lied, holding herself still so she didn't shake from the chill that engulfed her.

Tell was silent, watching her through narrow, assessing eyes, no longer silvery, but a hard steel-gray. Molly forced herself to meet his gaze. After a moment, he shrugged and flicked off the flashlight.

"Save the battery," he murmured.

The rain steadily assaulted the tent, its noise a soothing steady pattern. The air was growing cooler and the last vestiges of daylight faded.

Molly settled in the spot she was in and tried to see Tell in the darkness. She could barely make out his shape. Her legs were growing cold. She'd been stupid to pull completely away.

"So tell me more about being shunted around as a child," Tell invited.

"There's not much to tell. I didn't have the fun childhood you did."

Molly remembered being terrified when her mother died. Who'd take care of her, who'd ever love her again? She'd only been eight and left all alone. Her mother often worried aloud about their fate, money had been so scarce and hard to come by. She'd often told Molly she didn't know where their next meal would come from.

Molly knew now that her mother shouldn't have burdened a young child with her fears.

"So who had the most influence on your life?" Tell asked.

"Probably my mother. I learned security's the most important thing in life. And I need a plan to get it and keep it and not get pulled down by circumstances. That I learned from my early years and what happened when there was no security."

Her voice was calm, matter-of-fact. Not for anything would she let Tell know of the hurt and despair she'd felt all those years. The ongoing fear of not having a place to stay, food to eat. Of never knowing the love she'd felt from her mother.

She was making it on her own, but she knew that. If she wish to marry some day, she'd have to find a man who could provide for her and any children they might have, not someone like her father, a charming man, unskilled at anything but having a good time.

Or so her mother had always said. When he died, he left nothing but debts. They had been married so young. Neither had education or training beyond a high school diploma.

Molly wouldn't repeat her parents" mistake. Much as she was drawn to Tell, she couldn't risk her future for a charming, drifting cowboy, who didn't even have enough money to stay in a cheap motel.

The rain was slowing. Molly cocked her head. Maybe it'd stop soon. Let her get back to the hotel, back to her quiet life, end this craziness with her Texas cowboy. She shouldn't have come. She was tempting fate.

"That explains your desire to marry a rich man," Tell said softly.

"I don't want to marry a rich man," she said sharply, "That's not my goal in life. If I marry I want it to be a man who has a steady income, a skill that can be counted on. I don't want to be left destitute if he dies or if I die young leave any children in the circumstances I was."

"So show your bank balance to the lady before she will become involved." His voice had a hard edge.

"You're deliberately taking this wrong. I don't need to see anyone's bank book, but I want to know there's security. This is the same argument we had the other night. You can't see my point of view. Why would you? You have parents still living, cousins, aunts, uncles, grandparents. Sounds like an entire town of relatives. Even if they each put you up once a week, you had security of knowing you were with family. I have no one. Only myself."

"Do you want to see my bank book?"

"Do you have one?"

Sarcasm dripped from her tone. He judged her and found her wanting. Too bad. She was who she was and knew what she needed in her life to have to find peace.

"Not on me, but I can get it sent here," he bit out.

"Don't bother. I'm sure you're nicely situated, for a cowboy. What will you do when you get old? I've never seen old cowboys. Do they have retirement homes for them?"

Tell sat up and moved towards her.

"You may not live to see anyone old with a sharp tongue like yours. I'll make out just fine, darlin''. The rain's stopped—let's go."

He reached for her in the dark and drew her towards the flap. Thrusting it open, Molly grabbed her glasses. In seconds the two of them stood on the damp grass of the meadow. The air was crystal-clear and clean. The wind had died. The night was black as pitch, the last of the clouds obscuring the stars.

Tell switched on the flashlight and ran the light over her. She blinked in the sudden brightness and turned slightly. As the light traveled the length of her, she looked down.

The shirt covered her to mid-thigh, the sleeves hung down below her wrists, even rolled up. It covered more of her than her lacy white cover-up, but she felt vulnerable. It was Tell's shirt. There was a certain intimacy implied in wearing his clothes.

"Come on." His voice was impersonal, impatient.

Tell strode off ahead and Molly reached for her glasses and damp clothes, then hurried to keep up, not wanting to get too far behind and lose the light.

He used a towel to wipe off the seats and climbed into the driver's seat.

"I'll drive. Toss me the keys."

They returned to Acapulco in silence. Tell spoke only when asking her to open and close the wooden gate. Molly complied, afraid even to suggest he do it himself. He seemed to be in a black mood, but she couldn't help that. Let him think her a gold-digger. After today she doubted she'd ever see him again.

He drew up beside a black Ford sedan.

"This is my car. I'll follow you to Las Casitas D'Oro to make sure you get back safely."

She nodded, wanting to apologize, wanting things to be different. But she'd already said things she couldn't recall and nothing would really change even if she could.

She drove carefully back to the hotel, conscious of the twin lights behind her, of Tell watching out for her. She felt safe, cherished. She wished things had been different, wished he had money and a steady job so she could let herself fall in love...

What was she thinking of? She couldn't wish for the moon and have everything come her way. It never had. She was no longer a little girl wishing for a fairy-tale life. She was grown and realistic.

Tell was not for her. He'd never given any indication of wanting anything more than a light dalliance while on vacation. He'd picked her up in the casita's pool area. He was probably as disappointed she wasn't some rich tourist as she was he wasn't gainfully employed.

She had better remember that and let herself be guided appropriately.

When Molly reached her room, she heard Beverley talking in the adjacent room, dictating again. Tomorrow she'd be back to work.

And Molly was relieved. It'd give her something to do and take her mind off Tell Hardin.

Seven

Despite Molly's belief in reality, she slept in Tell's shirt, imagining he was wrapped around her as the soft blue denim was. When she awoke the next morning, she felt lonely and sad. She wished she could let go of her need for security, grab what happiness life might offer and look forward to the future without worry or fear.

But she couldn't. She had to make sure she'd be better prepared for whatever came her way than her mother had been. At least if something happened to her at a young age, there was no small child to leave alone in the world.

She walked out on to the patio promptly at eight. Beverley was already sitting beside the pool, sipping a cup of the rich coffee the hotel provided. She smiled brightly at Molly.

"All rested and ready for work?"

Molly smiled back, glad that routine would take over. She'd had too much time off. Work was safer. She sank on a chair near the table and reached for a cup.

"Sure am. Did I hear you dictating last night?"

"Yes, I was on a roll and didn't finish until late. I have about three tapes for you to get started on and can do several more today. I know just what I'm going to reveal about Pershing today and can't wait to get started. He was such an interesting man—I don't think everyone knows that and I hope I can help some people discover that fact."

She nodded in time with her speaking and Molly was again reminded of a little bird.

"Tonight, though, we're taking a break. I know it's dull for you here, with no friends and all. The Alverado family has invited us to dinner. They're old friends of mine. You'll like them. They have a son and daughter about your age, so you'll meet some young people. Maybe have a chance to go somewhere."

It was on the tip of Molly's tongue to tell Beverley about her meeting Tell, but she held back. Beverley had been very specific that she didn't think Molly should have anything to do with Tell Hardin.

And Molly didn't want to take the chance of upsetting her boss by telling her she hadn't listened to her advice.

Besides, after last night, Tell wouldn't want to see her again.

"I don't really have anything to wear to a dinner party," Molly said softly, thinking of the practical clothes she'd brought and the new casual ones she'd bought.

"Well, we'll take a break this afternoon and you can dash down to the little shop near the lobby. They have some nice dresses."

Which would cost the earth, Molly thought. Her funds were meager now and she wasn't to be paid for another few days.

She'd look, anyway. If she couldn't find anything, she'd tell Beverley she couldn't go.

When she'd finished eating, Molly went to get the tapes from Beverley. Sitting before the computer, she was soon caught up in the life and times of General Black Jack Pershing.

Several times during the morning, Molly's mind wandered and end up thinking about Tell. She'd see his face before her, his dancing gray eyes, his mocking smile.

Then she'd remember the kisses he'd given her at the beach

and she'd grow warm, distracted. He filled her thoughts. It was hard to marshal them in other directions.

Shaking her head to clear it, she'd attack the work furiously, trying to forget. But sooner or later her mind would remember.

"Are you all right?" Beverley asked at one point, looking at her strangely.

Molly looked up, flushed. She hadn't heard her employer enter her room. She nodded, wary of further questions.

"You looked distracted." Beverley watched her secretary from her dark eyes. "Not getting sick, Montezuma's revenge?"

"No, I'm fine." Molly tried to concentrate on the words in her ears, transcribing them to the computer. She wouldn't think of Tell again.

After a light lunch of salad, crackers and iced tea, Molly returned to work. She'd take a break when the stores opened after siesta and see if the shop near the lobby had anything she could afford. She set herself a goal of two more tapes finished by then. Forcing herself to concentrate, she didn't think of Tell all afternoon—until she started walking towards the shop.

Wondering what kind of dress she might be able to afford, she fantasized about buying a beautiful dress that would drive Tell wild with desire and passion. It'd be nice to have him see her all dressed up, instead of in the resort attire or the business suit from Los Angeles.

But her dream faded as she looked at the dresses on the racks. It was as she feared. They were very expensive, some of them hundreds of dollars. There were few in her size and all too expensive for her purse.

It was fun to look at them, to imagine Tell seeing her wear them. What would his reaction be?

"Can I help you, senorita?" The assistant was elegantly dressed, unlike those clerks in the shops along the Avenida Costera Miguel Alameda. Much better dressed than Molly could afford to be.

"I was looking for a dress to wear to a dinner party, but everything here cost more than I care to spend," she said, moving dresses on the rod.

"Our selection in your size is quite limited, unfortunately. There is an excellent shop in the Continental Hotel; perhaps they'd have something for you."

Molly smiled. "My time's limited. I'm working and was hoping to dash in and find something."

She looked past the assistant and then saw the dress for her. It was as blue as the sky over Acapulco, with a halter neck, fitted bodice and a flaring skirt. It was hanging over a rack by the register.

"How about that one? Is it in my size?" Molly knew it'd be way too expensive, yet it was perfect.

"Oh, que lastima, it is ripped. We are not selling it. It is a beautiful gown, si?"

The woman brought it over to Molly, who touched the silky material, loving the feel of it. She could see the tear, on the skirt, on the side.

"It could be mended," she said softly, reaching for it to hold it in front of her. She moved before the mirror. Her eyes sparkled, their color enhanced by the soft blue of the dress. Her cheeks were rosy, her lips glossy.

She wished Tell could see her in this dress.

"We do not sell goods that need to be mended." The assistant was kind.

"I'd buy it and fix it. It would be a wonderful dress to have. Please."

The woman hesitated.

"It's good business to make some money, even if it's not as much as you'd have made had the dress not been ripped," Molly pressed.

"You are correct, senorita, some money is better than a loss. Si, I will sell it to you."

Molly almost hugged herself with glee as she walked back up the hill to the casita. The dress had been discounted to one-third the original price. It had still cost more than Molly usually spent on a dress, but had been affordable. A few minutes with a needle and thread and it'd be perfect.

Molly flew through the work remaining, anticipation building for the evening ahead. She'd meet Beverley's friends, enjoy herself. It'd be nice to get out and see some of the real Mexico, instead of the tourist spots.

She longed to see Tell, but told herself that would be pointless. He'd just laugh at her anyway, all dressed up.

But she wished that he could see her in the pretty dress, just once.

The dress fit as though it had been made with her in mind. The halter neck bared her arms and shoulders, her creamy tanned skin a perfect foil. It was low in the back, but hugged her waist like a second skin. The skirt flared around her legs, skimming the tops of her knees.

Putting on her make-up carefully, Molly decided to leave her glasses at home. She could see well enough to avoid running into anything and wouldn't be so self-conscious if she couldn't see all the people at the party.

The real reason, of course, was glasses ruined the effect of the dress.

When she and Beverley arrived at the Alverado villa, Molly was struck by its size. Easily twice the size of an average house in the US, it was situated on a bluff overlooking Acapulco Bay. The front windows framed the view as though a fine artist had positioned it. The lights were coming on in homes and buildings across the water and the scene was breathtaking.

She wished for a moment she'd worn her glasses to see the

view properly.

There were already about a dozen people gathered on the front patio, a uniformed waiter circulated with glasses of champagne. More people were arriving behind them. Molly had thought it a quiet dinner among friends, not a party. She spoke no Spanish–would she be able to communicate at all?

"Beverley, it's so good to see you."

A tall, distinguished gentleman approached them, giving her a kiss on each cheek. Beverley smiled up and greeted him.

"Juan, I'd like to present Molly Spencer. She's my new assistant." Holding up the arm in a cast, she grimaced. "Next best thing to typing myself," she said with a friendly smile at Molly.

"Welcome, Senorita Spencer. Mi casa es tu casa." He bowed in a courtly manner.

Molly smiled shyly. "How do you do? I was afraid for a moment I would be unable to communicate. I don't speak Spanish."

"It is of no matter. Most of the guests here tonight will speak some English. I assure you that we will have someone with you who can translate, should you wish to converse with anyone who cannot speak English. I'm happy you came."

He turned and searched the crowd, calling when he found the man he wanted. "Luis."

A young man excused himself from the group he was with and moved gracefully towards Juan. Tall dark and suavely handsome, Molly was taken with his good looks. The suit he wore made him all the more distinguished.

"Luis, I'd like to present Molly Spencer, an associate of our friend Beverley. Senorita Spencer does not speak Spanish. Perhaps you could introduce her around and make sure she is looked after." The older man smiled at Molly. "Luis is my son."

"Si, Papa, my pleasure. How do you do, Senorita Spencer?"

"Very well, thank you."

Molly briefly studied the young man before her. He was slim, tall, and quite immaculately turned out. His eyes were dark brown and friendly. He smiled and offered her his arm.

Taking it, Molly stepped beside him and they began walking around the reception area. Molly was introduced to almost everyone there. When they'd completed the introductions he felt necessary, Luis took her to the far edge of the patio and seated her at one of the tables.

"Duty done, I can now devote the rest of the evening to you. What would you like to drink? A Planter's Punch, perhaps?"

"What's that?"

"Fruit juices with nun—light, refreshing."

"I'd like to try it, it sounds good."

She felt a flush of embarrassment she didn't even know what to ask for. She looked around when he left. The large patio had a low stone wall surrounding it, also providing space for people to sit as she saw a couple doing. Lights were strung to illuminate the area without glaring in anyone's eyes. Several tables and chairs were occupied, three still empty.

Luis was back in only moments, two tall glasses in his hand. When Molly sipped hers, she smiled.

"It's delicious."

"Bueno. Now tell me all about you, Senorita Spencer. You have not been long with Beverley or I would have met you before this."

"No, just the last several weeks. And it's temporary until her broken wrists heals."

"How do you like working with her?"

Molly lost her shyness around Luis and found it easy to talk with him. She liked her job and was easily persuaded to talk about it. And about her liking for Mexico.

"It's beautiful here; is all your country so lovely?"

"I, of course, think so. We have a home in Mexico City as well. There's a different beauty there, still lovely, but I prefer the beach."

Molly smiled, knowing that'd be her preference if she lived in a house with a view like this one.

"Have you seen much of Acapulco?" Luis asked, his eyes studying the pretty girl across from him, never distracted by the other guests circulating.

"I have seen the beaches and some of the sightseeing places, old town, the cathedral, La Quebrada."

Talking about her tour brought Tell to mind.

Without meaning to do so, Molly found herself comparing Luis to Tell. The man before her was obviously wealthy, accustomed to fine things. The house was exquisitely decorated, with valuable objects d'art, expensive Persian rugs and fine furniture. Luis's clothes were tailored to perfection. He wore a gold ring on his right hand and the Rolex at his wrist was costly.

Yet, charming and attentive as Luis was, Molly missed Tell.

She'd rather have him sitting across from her, with his mocking eyes, as she took in all the beauty of Luis's home. He'd put her firmly in her place, scoff at her for being impressed with riches, and be so devastatingly attractive that she'd lose sight of any other man in the room.

"What are you thinking, Molly? Your face is very expressive." Luis smiled kindly.

She colored slightly and looked away. Tell had told her the same thing.

Across the room she spotted a tall man dressed in a dark suit. For a second she thought it was Tell. Then a couple of baseball devotees wandered between them, arguing about a score, and she looked away. Great, now she was imagining she saw him everywhere. What would Tell be doing at the

Alvarado's"? She glanced back at Luis and smiled.

"I was thinking how lovely your view is. Would a person ever grow tired with this view, ever take it for granted?"

She hoped that'd cover her momentary distraction.

Luis swung around to look at it and turned back to tell her of how his grandfather had first built the villa, long before Acapulco was world-famous, how his family had always spent winters and fiesta-time in Acapulco.

Molly was content to listen to him talk, learn something of how a Mexican family lived. As the evening progressed, she periodically searched the other guests, but didn't see the tall man again.

"I'm about ready to leave—how are you doing?" Beverley hurried over to Molly, smiling brightly at Luis.

"Why don't you take Molly out, Luis? She's getting bored sitting around with an old lady like me. She needs to get out and meet some young people, enjoy the night life in Acapulco."

"Oh, no. I'm fine, really," Molly protested, laughing nervously. "I've seen lots of the sights. Luis doesn't have to bother..."

"Ah, but it would be no bother; it would give me great pleasure. Perhaps dinner the evening after tomorrow? We can go to one of the clubs in town when we finish eating. It would be my pleasure."

"Oh, I don't think...the work and all." Molly knew it was a lame excuse.

"Nonsense. Of course she can go. Come to Las Casitas D'Oro about eight, Luis. I'll see she's ready. We're near the top, Casita 284. Lovely to see you again. Do you want to stay a while longer, Molly?"

"No, I'm ready when you are."

Things were going too fast for her. She didn't want to go out with Luis, didn't want him to feel obliged to take her out.

But how could she get out of it when he and Beverley only meant to be kind?

She'd have to go.

And she'd rather not.

Luis was nice, but he wasn't anyone special. She'd had a pleasant evening tonight, but didn't need to be wined and dined by Luis.

She refused to think what she'd rather be doing. And with whom.

The next two days were idyllic. Molly rose early and ate breakfast on the patio overlooking the large blue bay. Two cruise ships came in, their horns loud in the morning stillness. She watched them dock and imagined the flurry of activity on board as everyone prepared to visit Acapulco.

Trying to keep up with Beverley was hard. The woman talked constantly, tape recorder in hand, dictating tape after tape. Molly's speed increased, her accuracy increased, and still she fell behind.

When she took a break, she'd swim, lie in the sun and dream about Tell Hardin. She hadn't seen nor heard from him since the night of the rainstorm. She knew she made him mad with her desire for security, but still wanted to see him again.

Was this how she would feel when they left Acapulco and she'd never even have the chance to see him again?

The second day she finished work and took another quick swim before beginning her preparations for the evening's dinner. She wore the blue halter dress again, she wasn't going to spend any more money on frivolous dresses. Once again she wished Tell could see her wearing it. She was a fool to keep remembering him; she'd do better to cultivate someone like Luis. He had charm, looks, manners and money. What more could a woman want in a mate?

By the time dinner was halfway over, Molly had her answer. She wanted excitement.

Luis was nice, kind, polite, charming. But he wasn't interesting to her.

His talk of his work in the city was boring. She didn't care about Mexico City nor the businesses there. She was only visiting this country. She'd be going home soon. She didn't care about the coups he'd pulled off, or the large deals he was working on.

Money still played an important part of her decision for a life partner, but some and a common interest would also have to be present.

The rest of the evening passed pleasantly enough. They finished dinner and went to Baby-O, one of the frolicking clubs that came to life after dark. Dancing eliminated the ability to think and Molly had a fine time. It was late when they reached the hotel.

"Thank you, Luis. I enjoyed myself," she said politely as she prepared to leave his car.

"It was my pleasure. Unfortunately, I am leaving for Mexico City in the morning—that deal I was telling you about. It may be some time before I can return to Acapulco. May I call you when I do?"

"If we're still here. I don't know exactly how long Beverley plans to stay."

She was grateful for the reprieve. With any luck he'd forget about contacting her or they'd suddenly return to the States.

"I will call as soon as I know my plans," he said.

He walked her to her door, kissed her lightly on her cheek and bade her a pleasant goodnight.

Molly smiled as she let herself into her room. The evening had been enjoyable enough, but if Luis didn't return from

Mexico City before they left she wouldn't be disappointed. He was charming company and made sure she'd had a good time. But she had no strong desire to spend any more time with him.

Molly switched on her lights and dropped her bag on her bed. Walking to the sliding glass door she pulled it open. She'd take a quick look over the bay before retiring. It was a view she never tired of and wanted to store up memories for the long years ahead. She'd probably never return to Acapulco.

From habit her eyes went to the far corner—and stopped when she saw Tell lounging in one of the chairs.

"Tell?"

She darted a glance to the room next to hers. It was dark. Had Beverley gone to sleep? The curtain was drawn—maybe so.

Quickly Molly walked around the pool over to where Tell sat watching her. "What are you doing here?"

"Hello, Molly." He remained seated, looking out over the bay.

"What are you doing here?" Her heart soared.

"I brought your souvenirs back. You left them at the camp when we left." He motioned to the plastic bag on the table near him. "I thought I'd say hi. I've been here for hours."

"I was out."

She sat on the edge of the chair nearest him and looked at him in the dim light.

"Dinner and dancing by the looks of it." He turned to run his gaze over her.

She'd worn the blue dress again and was glad Tell could see her in. Would he think it suited her?

"Yes, with someone who invited me and paid for the both of us," she snapped.

She didn't want to talk about her evening with Luis. She knew Tell would think the worst.

101

"Who with?"

"A friend of Beverley's. Luis Alverado."

"Well, well, well, so the little personal assistant did all right for herself."

His taunting voice hit her like a fist.

Molly felt her anger rise. "What do you mean?"

"Luis Alverado's quite a catch. I bet you never even asked to see his bank balance. He shows off his wealth all the time."

"I didn't go out with him for that," she said.

She knew he'd get it wrong.

"Of course you did, why else?"

"Beverley wanted me to have a good time and suggested I go out with him."

"And have you been having an awful time?"

"No. I...but she doesn't know I've seen you a couple of times."

"That's right, we don't want to go against her wishes. She might fire you and then where would you be?"

"Where I don't expect to be. I'm working hard at this job and I think I can keep it."

"Unless Beverley finds out you're seeing me, after she said you shouldn't," he said relentlessly.

Molly looked away, suddenly depressed.

It was true; how would Beverley react to the fact Molly had been seeing this man behind her back? She still didn't know Beverley well enough to judge her reactions to Molly's ignoring her advice. Would she laugh and pass it off or become angry?

Tell sighed and rose.

"Where are you going?" Molly stood. She'd longed to see him for two days; surely he wasn't leaving already.

"Back to camp. I brought your things. That's all I came for."

"Don't go. How's your foot?" She desperately wanted him

to stay a while longer. She reached out and took his arm, feeling the warmth of his skin against her palm.

"Healing. Why should I stay?"

He stepped closer to her, tilted her head up to his gaze.

"No glasses? Luis rated special attention. Did he find you beautiful and ravishing?"

"He said I looked nice."

Molly could scarcely speak above the tightness in her throat as she gazed into the shimmering silver of his eyes. His hand at her chin heated her skin, her knees grew weak. She longed to reach out to him for support.

"Nice is too insipid for you, my proper little darlin'". How were his kisses, hot like mine? Or gentle and polite?"

"He only kissed me on the cheek," she whispered, drowning in his gaze, her spirits rising. Was he jealous of Luis?

"More fool he," Tell said as he lowered his mouth to hers, holding back as his lips touched hers, as if he waited for a signal from her.

Molly moved against him, encircling his neck with her arms and pressing herself against the length of his hard body.

He held her tightly against him and deepened the kiss. Molly thought she'd might explode.

She could scarcely breathe, sensations threatening to overwhelm her. She could only feel Tell, the thickness of his hair, the hot passion of his mouth, the wild beating of his heart against hers. His hands moving over her bare back, caressing her, pressing her closer.

He swept her into his arms and started across the patio. For a moment Molly thought to stop him, but then changed her mind.

For one magical night she'd sleep in his arms. She knew she couldn't build a life with him, but she'd at least have one magical night. All thoughts of security fled. She wanted him, he wanted her. She'd sort things out in the morning.

Eight

Tell set her on her feet on the terrazzo floor of her room. Molly blinked up at him in the bright room light. He stood just inside the door, his tanned chest rising and falling as if he'd been running. Molly felt better knowing she wasn't the only one affected by their kisses.

The sudden rap on the door startled her. She dropped her arms and spun around. Who could it be at this time of night? She peered at her clock; it looked as if it was after midnight.

Tell stepped up beside her, leaning over to speak softly in her ear.

"Who is it?"

"I don't know."

The rap came again. "Molly? Are you in there?"

It was Beverley Sampson.

"Blast it." Tell breathed. He kissed Molly on the cheek. "You've got to let her in." He moved back out of the sliding door.

Molly walked to the front door of her room and opened.

"I was hoping you were back and hadn't just left the light on. I left my purse at one of the places I stopped in tonight and didn't have my key. I didn't want to have to drive all the way back down tonight and when I saw your bathroom light on I hoped you'd be home. Did you and Luis have a good time? You can't have been home long—you're still dressed."

Beverley bustled into Molly's room and sank on the chair.

"I've only been home for a few minutes," Molly said, darting a swift glance towards the patio.

She didn't see Tell. He'd probably left. Molly's lips felt swollen from Tell's kisses. Could Beverley see that? And if she did, would she think it was from Luis?

"Well, I hope you don't mind me sleeping in with you tonight. I don't know where I left my purse and I hate to have to go down to the lobby. This'll make the third key I've lost and they get so tiresome when they have to issue new keys. There's always the worry thieves got mine and could access the room at any time.

You have a big bed— we can share, can't we?"

Molly's heart dropped as she sank down on the edge of the king size bed Beverley spoke of. Only moments ago, she'd thought to share it with Tell. She wondered if Tell was in hearing distance. And how he must be laughing if he was.

"Sure, it's a big bed. I have an extra nightie that'll fit you, too." Molly smiled.

There was no help for it. Maybe it was fate's way of stepping in and making sure she didn't make a mistake.

When Beverley went into the bathroom to change and prepare for bed, Molly slipped out to the patio.

Tell was leaning against the far wall. She walked over to him.

"I guess you heard," she said.

He smiled down at her and drew a finger along her jaw.

"Yeah, I heard. Her timing stinks. Want to come back with me to my camp?" he asked, his eyes mocking her. He already knew the answer.

She smiled back at him, knowing he was teasing her. Slowly she shook her head

She wanted him to visit her again, but didn't voice it aloud. Silently she stood and watched him.

"You'd better get back inside. I'll see you," he said, brushing his fingers against her cheek again.

"You'll come again?" she ventured, unable to help herself.

"One of these days. You want to go riding along the beach?"

"I don't know when I'll have a day off again."

"Just let Miguel know."

She felt disappointed. She'd thought he'd come by to find out if she were free. But maybe he had other plans. The feeling left her sad, frustrated, unsettled.

"Goodnight, Molly." He leaned over and kissed her softly.

Like the first night, he faded into the darkness. She couldn't hear him leave, but knew he was gone. Slowly she returned to her bedroom and soon to bed.

"Luis is so charming, I always thought," Beverley said the next morning as they shared croissants and coffee on the patio. The day was bright and warm. It'd grow hot before the sun was much higher. There was no breeze to temper the heat.

Molly didn't want to think about Luis Alverado. She'd much rather remember Tell's kisses of last night, the feel of his hands against her skin and the delight she'd thought they'd share.

In the bright light of day she was relieved she hadn't given in to the passion that had built between them. If she had half a brain, she'd curtail her involvement with him totally. He was not for her.

He'd never suggested he was. All along he'd been up front with her. He was on what appeared an endless vacation. He obviously had very little money, camping out when he could have enjoyed the amenities of a reasonably priced hotel in town.

The future was too uncertain to trust in a man who had no prospects. Who, instead of saving his money, spent money on frivolous vacations, on self-indulgent fun. Such a man as her father had been.

She told herself this over and over, but she still yearned for Tell Hardin.

Was this how her mother felt about her father?

"Are you seeing him again?" Beverley asked, her head cocked in interest.

"Who?" Molly blinked at her. Did she mean Tell?

"Luis, my dear."

"I don't think so. He's going to Mexico City today and may not be back here in Acapulco for a long time. I wasn't sure how much longer we'd be here."

"Another few weeks, I'm sure. We're halfway through the first draft. I'll finish that and then we can see about heading for another location. I like to take a break between writing and the editing process. The book seems fresher when I've been away from it a few days. Maybe I'll check in at home to see how things are going there. Then perhaps we could travel up to Canada, stay in Banff. I have friends there, too. And summers in Canada are lovely."

"I believe you have friends all over," Molly said with a smile. She enjoyed seeing how Beverley lived her life.

"I do like meeting new people and seeing new places. I think you have to live in a place a while to get the feel of it, don't you?"

Molly nodded, but wondered how authentic her view of Mexico was living in a luxurious hotel. A flat in town would be more authentic.

Not that she would trade staying here for anything. It was wonderful.

It might be wonderful, but there was still work to be done. Molly typed all day, Beverley showing no signs of flagging. Between tapes, Molly took a couple of breaks to swim and lie in the sun briefly, wondering where else a secretary could take breaks in a private pool and immediately resume work with a cover-up over her swimsuit. She surely had the best job in the world.

In the evening, she was still at the computer, trying to catch up with Beverley's dictation. The woman could go on and on, and Molly was hard pressed to keep up. It didn't look as if Beverley was reaching another period where she couldn't write. Exactly when Molly wanted another day off. A day to ride with Tell.

Day after day, Beverley dictated almost non stop while Molly frantically transcribed to keep up.

At night she dreamed of Tell. He didn't come round and Molly didn't contact Miguel. There was no message to pass on. She didn't know when she'd have a day available.

She wondered what Tell was doing during the time she didn't see him. Had he found another girl on vacation to take around, one who was out for a good time?

Or were things so tight that he couldn't afford much and was saving until such time they could be together?

They could still go Dutch. He'd seemed determined on that the day they'd gone sightseeing. Molly smiled remembering their afternoon. And the meal at his camp. She smiled a lot in remembering things about Tell. She wished he were–

Back to typing. No use dreaming dreams that would never be. She'd learned that in her childhood.

At last the day she'd been waiting for arrived. Beverley walked into her room in the afternoon and dropped a tape on the desk.

"That's it. I'm exhausted, totally dried up. I can't write

another word until I recharge my batteries. I don't want anyone to even mention Black Jack Pershing to me. I want to forget I ever heard about the man." She ran her hands through her short hair.

Molly's heart leaped. She'd have her day with Tell after all. She'd finish tonight. Tomorrow she'd be free.

"I thought I'd take a short trip to Taxco and see the silver they have up there; they're famous for it, you know. Do you want to come with me?" Beverley invited.

"I was thinking of going riding on the beach on my next day off," Molly said tentatively, hoping Beverley wouldn't ask for details.

"Good idea. I haven't done that in ages. I wish I could with you. It's no fun to do things by yourself all the time. Though you haven't complained once. You do your job well and find entertainment for yourself when we're not working. It's refreshing. Riding sounds fun. I was raised on a ranch, you know."

Molly held her breath.

She was pleased Beverley liked her performance, but she didn't want Beverley to go riding with her. She wanted to go with Tell.

But she couldn't tell Beverley that without answering a lot of questions. Beverley had warned her off. What would she say if she discovered Molly was seeing him? She might not be so pleased about that.

Beverley fell silent for a moment, gazing out over the view. "No, I think I'll keep to my original plan and go to Taxco. I've already arranged for a driver. Are you sure you don't want to come?"

Molly let her breath out slowly, unaware that she'd been holding it. She smiled and shook her head.

"Thanks, but I think I'll just stay around here."

She was anxious to see Miguel, let him send a message that she would have free time tomorrow. He was her only way to contact Tell.

"I'm sorry Luis had to leave for Mexico City, He could have shown you around. His family's lived here for years as well as having a lovely home in Mexico City. He's quite a catch." Beverley smiled slyly at Molly, her bright eyes twinkling in excitement.

"I'm really not looking for a catch," Molly said slowly, her eyes on her computer. "He's very nice–"

"But he doesn't excite you. Well, there'll be other men. I know a few, actually, who might get your heart racing."

"You're not trying to set me up with anyone, are you? What would you do until your wrist heal? You need me."

"You're right. Perish the thought. I like the work you do, Molly. Stay away from all men."

Beverley laughed and patted Molly on the shoulder. She drifted from the room, and Molly began typing frantically.

How long before she could take a walk and talk to Miguel? How could she casually leave and not have Beverley suspect anything?

Would she even notice? Or was Molly just self-conscious because of her guilty conscience?

Guilty conscience? She'd done nothing to feel guilty about. Beverley had suggested she stay away from Tell, but only because he was trouble. Molly was only seeing him to pass the time when available. He meant nothing beyond that.

What about the other evening? Had Beverley not arrived when she did, Tell would have been considerably more than just a casual friend to while away her free time.

Molly's cheeks burned in remembrance. His kisses were intoxicating, his very touch heated her skin, made rational thought impossible. But the other night had surely been crazy, not to be repeated.

The hours dragged by slowly as each moment Molly longed to fly to Miguel and have him contact Tell. But she diligently transcribed the tapes Beverley dictated. It was late afternoon before she'd allow herself the break she'd been longing for.

Casually she stretched and moved to the patio. Beverley wasn't in sight. Molly didn't wait.

She was disappointed when she discovered that Miguel was not on duty. A young man named Carlos stood behind the desk.

"Miguel will be on duty tomorrow," he told her.

"Oh, but he's to give a message to someone for me. Will he be around later today?"

"No, senorita, today is his day off. He will not be back until morning."

Molly's heart sank. She nodded, and turned away, tears threatening.

She'd so counted on having Miguel contact Tell. She'd never thought he might not be here. And she couldn't remember where Tell's camp was. Would it do any good to go into Acapulco and see if he was on the beach?

There would be hundreds of people on the beach—she'd never find one tall, ruggedly cowboy among all the sunbathers.

She'd have to wait until tomorrow. Disappointment swept through her. She'd been so counting on seeing him, on riding with him once Beverley told her she wouldn't be working. What if Beverley was ready to work again the following day?

The evening proved long and lonely for Molly. She finished transcribing all the tapes, double-checked her work and sat out on the balcony well into the night gazing at the bright lights encircling the bay. She hoped Tell would come as he had before. But he did not.

As soon as Beverley left the next morning for her trip to Taxco, Molly walked down to the concierge's desk. Miguel was on duty and she asked him to contact Tell for her. Returning to her room, Molly opened her sliding door to make sure she didn't miss Tell's arrival, if he came. She dressed quickly in her bikini. She'd sunbathe to while the hours away. With anticipation rising, she lay on the lounger beside the pool. How long before he came?

The morning passed. The sun reached its zenith. Molly moved to the shade offered by the umbrella, changing her chair so that she could gaze over the sparkling waters of Acapulco Bay.

The spanking white cruise ship sailing into the harbor drew her eye. Its horns blew, joyfully announcing its arrival. Molly could imagine the excitement of the tourists as they lined the deck, eyes drinking in the beauty of the scene. In only moments, they'd be flooding the gangplank, and spilling out into Acapulco to sample its beaches, shops, restaurants and, later, its nightlife.

For a moment, she envied them. She glanced again over her shoulder to the empty hillside. There was no sign of Tell. Had he got her message? Had he changed his mind about wanting to see her again? Was he coming?

She closed her eyes and settled back on the lounger, concentrating on the warmth that reflected from the patio, the soft air that caressed her skin as she dozed in the shade. She heard the murmur of the hotel landscapers in the background, the soft hum of the pool's filter. Soon she fell asleep.

It was mid-afternoon when Molly awoke. She looked around for Tell, disappointed when she didn't see him, but resigned now.

Miguel probably needed to get off duty and drive to Tell's camp to give him a message. Tell probably hadn't a clue she'd sent him one. She'd get something to eat and do something else for the rest of the afternoon, not just sit and wait for a man who obviously wasn't coming.

She donned her cover-up and stuffed a book and hat into her bag. Wandering down to the lobby, she'd catch a ride to the beach club, where she could eat from the buffet, snorkel in the sheltered pools and read her book. She'd have people around her, even if she didn't want to talk to them. It was better than remaining in her room.

Miguel was on duty. Molly went to inquire about the shuttle service to the beach club.

"In only another ten minutes, senorita, the bus leaves. It returns every half-hour."

"Thank you." She hesitated, then asked, "Did my message make it?"

She hated asking, but if he'd received the message then there was something that prevented his coming. Maybe he changed his mind.

"Si, senorita. It was delivered."

She nodded and smiled politely at him, turning away to await the shuttle bus. So Miguel had a way to deliver it even though he was working. She refused to speculate on why Tell hadn't come. Perhaps he no longer wanted to spend time with her.

Molly stayed at the club until dusk. She caught the bus back to the hotel, climbed the steep path to her room and heading straight for the shower. When finished, she donned her nightgown and light robe. She had started a good mystery and it would occupy her through the evening.

Ordering a salad from room service, she opened her door for the nice breeze. Standing in the doorway, her eyes moved around the patio, disappointed again.

Wait—on the table, a dark pile. She moved closer to see what it was, curiosity aroused.

Dark jeans were folded neatly on the table, and a white strip of paper showed beneath the folds. She picked them up and moved towards the light.

Had he come by? Had she missed him after all?

The handwriting was bold, large.

Pick you up at ten tomorrow. In case you don't have jeans, wear these. Wear bathing suit, no shirt necessary, but sun screen required. Tell

Excitement blossomed within Molly as a smile threatened to split her face. He'd come after all. And he wanted to see her tomorrow. At ten. She hugged the jeans against her chest, closing her eyes to better envision his dear face. Only a few more hours and she'd see him again.

Molly tried on the jeans first thing the next morning. They were only slightly loose, though long. Carefully, she rolled up the legs so that she could walk without tripping. She stood before the mirror, startled at the image that was reflected. Jeans that followed the line of her hips, a narrow waist and full breasts in a revealing pink bikini-top. Her eyes sparkled, and her cheeks were rosy with the sun and excitement. No way was she going to meet Tell Hardin looking like this.

She reached for her shirt. Buttoning it up, she looked more like a young woman going out to ride a horse. She had no boots, of course, but did put on a pair of tennis shoes.

Molly was ready long before the appointed time and could scarcely sit still waiting for the minutes to drag by.

Promptly at ten, there was a knock on the door. Molly flew to answer it, a bright smile on her face.

Tell's dark, handsome face smiled down at her as she flung the door wide. His gaze ran over her, dancing with amusement. The cowboy hat he wore shaded his face, but she could see his eyes.

"Didn't read all the note, huh?" he asked, reaching out to unfasten one button of her blouse.

"Tell."

Molly's hands captured his, stopping his movement, but not before he'd unfastened another button, his fingers leaving tantalizing tingles where they brushed her skin. She stepped back, away from his overwhelming presence.

"Molly."

He stepped closer, leaned over and brushed her lips lightly with his. "I said no shirt necessary. I want to see you riding in the warm sun in only your bathing suit. You need the jeans for protection, but not the top."

I do, too, she thought—protection from you. "We'll see how hot it is when we get there," she stalled.

"Ready?"

She nodded, and went back for her bag. She didn't know what to bring, but her wallet for identification, a towel and sun screen would be in order.

Tell seated her in his little rental car and climbed in the driver's side. Checking around the car for a minute, he hit the steering-wheel.

"Damn. I left my wallet back at the camp." His eyes met Molly's. "Can you lend me some money until later? It'll take ages to drive back to camp now. I reserved the horses for ten thirty—we'd be late if I have to go back to camp."

She dropped her eyes, afraid he'd see the disappointment and hurt she felt.

Yet why should she find it unexpected? She'd known all along he was a drifting cowboy, who couldn't even afford to stay in a cheap hotel. She'd set herself up for this, thinking it was a date. She could always say no and leave.

Or pay the rental, enjoy his company and riding on the beaches of Mexico. Without him, she'd never have had the nerve to go riding alone.

"Sure, I brought my wallet," she said softly, daring to look up to meet his eye.

"I'll pay you back."

She shrugged and turned to the window not wanting to hear false promises.

No amount of wishing or dreaming would change anyone.

Tell Hardin was who he was. One of the things that attracted Molly to Tell was his carefree, easy going, adventurous attitude. If he chose to live in the moment, do what he wanted and not worry about stability or security or the future, she couldn't change him.

She didn't really want to. She wished she could be more like him.

A day on the beach didn't make a lifetime commitment. She'd enjoy the time, the company and the event. A memory to cherish down the years.

"I'm looking forward to this," she confided as they reached the main road, turning away from Acapulco, towards the wilder open beaches of the Pacific.

"I am, too. Your boss let you off again, eh?"

"She's hit a writer's block again and went to see the silver at Taxco. She left yesterday." Molly didn't say she'd been free all day. He knew that. She suddenly hoped he'd never learn she'd spent her day alone, hoping he'd show up.

"Didn't she invite you?"

"Yes, but I—"

Too late Molly saw the trap. She didn't want him to know she'd forgone the trip to be with him.

"You what?"

"I... I thought riding might be fun."

He chuckled and reached over to take her hand in his.

"Molly, is it so hard to say you wanted to spend some time with me?"

She nodded, refusing to look his way.

"Why?" he asked softly.

"I shouldn't," she whispered.

"I like spending time with you," he said easily.

"But it'll be so hard to say goodbye."

She tried not to think about it.

"So we won't."

"Acapulco is a dream time. This isn't like real life. You're on vacation and I'm not working at a regular job. It'll end. You'll leave, I'll leave and it'll be goodbye."

"I'll come see you in LA."

She giggled, picturing him in his faded jeans riding an old horse down the LA freeways.

"I don't think they have many ranches in LA."

"So come visit me in Texas."

She turned to look at him in surprise.

"Do you have a place in Texas? I thought cowboys stayed in bunkhouses."

"I have a bed; you can share that with me," he said audaciously, slanting a look down at her.

Color stained her cheeks and she held his look as long as she could before dropping her gaze. Her heart pounded beneath her shirt, the images of them together danced before her eyes.

"Would we be the only two in the bunkhouse?" she asked.

Tell roared with laughter, his hand tightening on hers.

Molly smiled; his laughter was infectious. The whole thing was absurd, but fun to dream about.

"Ah, Molly, love, what shall I do about you?" His face sobered, his tone grew pensive. "What shall I do?"

Tell's attention focused on driving. The road dipped over the crest of the hills encircling Acapulco Bay and dropped down to run near the sea. Lush palms towered along the road, the dense shrubbery and green plants making a barrier to the view of the Pacific that was just beyond.

Silently they drove on until at last Tell turned into the drive of the Revolcadero beach. Towering on either side of the drive were two of the luxury hotels that pampered the rich and famous. The Acapulco Princess rose like an Aztec pyramid ten stories above the beach. To the left was the Pierre Marques, low and rambling and exclusive.

Tell drove past both and on to the beach, turning towards the south. Before long he stopped. To the land side, a corral of horses and an open stable, to the sea a magnificent white sandy beach, stretching south as far as Molly could see. There were few people in sight.

"I thought we'd ride south, have a picnic lunch, swim some and then come back," Tell said as he parked the car.

"Sounds wonderful. I brought a towel, and I have my suit on."

"And a shirt you don't need," he grumbled.

She smiled. "But it'll keep the sun off me, so I don't burn."

"You've gotten a good tan since you've been here. I don't think you'd burn."

He reached out to draw a finger down her cheek, follow along her jawline, drop lower, down her neck, to the edge of the shirt, trace the edge.

"Stop it. I want to go riding."

She snatched his finger away and turned to open her door.

"Me, too," he said softly. "Me, too."

Nine

Tell drew saddlebags from the back of the little rental car and smiled at Molly.

"I remembered the other things. I had a lunch fixed for us and the drinks are wrapped in towels to stay cool. Ready?"

She nodded, her tote in hand. Following him to the stables, she watched the way he moved effortlessly over the uneven ground. His jeans were low-slung, his shirt open, swinging back in the movement of his body. He wore old scuffed tennis shoes, but they looked out of place. She could picture him in boots striding along with that same easy way. His Stetson hat shaded his face from the sun. His foot looked like it had healed, he wasn't limping.

Tell waited for her at the entrance, taking her hand in his and walking her through the large airy stable to the back office.

"How well can you ride?" he asked.

"I'm not great, but I can stay on a horse."

At least she hoped so. It had been years since she'd ridden a horse. Courtesy of a friend from high school.

Tell discussed their plans with the man in the office and before long one of the stable boys brought out two horses, tying them in the cross ties, then turning to get the saddles.

"Can you saddle your own?" Tell asked, handing her the saddlebags.

"I guess I could." She looked dubious.

"I'll do it."

Molly stepped back out of the way and watched Tell toss a saddle the first horse. Like everything else he did, he made it look easy. In no time both were ready to ride.

He tied the saddlebags on his mount, her tote on the smaller horse that Molly would ride.

Leading them outside, he stopped.

"Up you go. I'll double-check your stirrups."

Molly mounted, the horse standing docilely as Tell checked the length of the stirrups.

"Too long. Move your leg, I'll shorten it."

He handed her the reins of both horses and moved to shorten the stirrup on her left side. Sliding his hand along the outside of her leg, he steered her foot into the stirrup. Molly felt the warmth of his touch through the thick cotton of the jeans, her skin tingling in awareness.

Tell moved to the other side, adjusted the stirrup and slid his hand along her leg between the saddle and her thigh. This time, he rubbed her leg softly, his fingers hot through the thick material, the tremors his touch caused threatening to engulf her. Her stomach felt like molten lava, her heart skipped a beat, and desire rose and threatened to drown her.

Afraid of her own feelings, she snatched at his hand and drew it away.

Molly was lost in the thin sliver glint of his eyes staring back at her. Conscious of his touch, she could scarcely think. Heat swept through her. The restless stamp of the horses" hoofs and the muffled roar of the surf jerked her back to awareness.

It was a moment in time she'd never forget.

Tell took his reins and mounted, leading the way slowly down towards the water's edge. Once on firmer sand, the horses seem eager to go and he started off at a trot. Molly kept pace with him. Soon they increased to a canter and splashed in the water the receding waves deposited.

The sun shone from a cloudless sky. The sea to their right was blue and clear, the waves breaking with regularity on the pristine sand. The spray kicked up by the horses evolved into millions of rainbow glistening drops, showering the riders, the horses, until everything was wet.

On and on they rode, veering away from sunbathers, surfers, other riders whose horses were tethered on the shore. Back to the firm packed sand. On and on across the endless beach.

Molly never wanted to stop. She could ride until they reached the South Pole. The deserted beach ahead beckoned, the horses were fresh and she was totally happy. The day was glorious. She didn't want anything to mar its perfection.

Tell drew up, slowing the horses to a walk. As they blew gently, and splashed in the water, Tell grinned at Molly. He looked younger, carefree, happy.

And as if he were born to ride horses. He looked as if he were a part of the animal, moving with him, sitting as a part of the horse, not separate as a rider. Molly took a couple of picture with her phone. Not that she needed them to remind her of the day. She'd never forget.

Tell reached for her phone and took some of her. He looked at them for a moment, and then handed back her phone.

She was smiling a lot today. Happiness bubbled just beneath the surface, and it was all she could do to contain it within her, having forgotten for the moment that it was her money paying for the rides.

"Want to stop? Swim a little, then eat?" he asked.

"Or we could keep riding forever," she said, still gazing longingly southwards.

"It'd get cold about Chile," he said dryly, pulling his mount to a stop.

"You're so practical."

"You don't usually accuse me of that."

He dismounted, reaching up to lift Molly down. "But you are always accusing me of something."

"That's not true."

She tried to remember; did she always accuse him of something?

"And arguing with me. If I suggest something, you always have another answer. You can't agree with me on anything," he said.

"That's not true."

He smiled at her. "It is. If I say the ocean is blue—"

She looked over to the sea. It was blue, a turquoise, teal-color blue. "Well, to be strictly accurate, it's more aqua or teal than a real blue blue."

He swatted her gently on the bottom. "See what I mean? Nothing I say gets a simple—yes, I agree."

Molly looked at him from under her lashes. "If you were to say you were a drifting cowboy who can charm the birds from the trees, I might agree." She met his gaze bravely, though she could scarcely believe she'd been so bold.

He looked down into her blue eyes, the amusement in his fading, the gray growing smoky. She took a deep breath, the air charged with tension.

"You'd still not agree. Anyway, it's not true. Tell me why you wore this shirt."

Molly stood still as his fingers unfastened the buttons one by one. By sheer will-power, the trembling she felt inside she kept inside, even when it threatened to take charge. She wouldn't let him know how his touch affected her.

Slowly he drew the shirt from her shoulders, down her

arms, his hands skimming her silky skin, dropping it carelessly on the sand.

She refused to meet his eyes, staring fixedly on the strong brown column of his throat.

"Well?"

She swallowed. It was awkward to talk about it. He was so open and carefree. Could he understand she was too reserved to go about practically unclothed.

"It seemed too... too...revealing," she ended in a whisper.

Tell chuckled softly, his finger beneath her chin, tilting her head to meet his gaze.

"Honey, you have the figure a man longs for, curves in the right places, long legs for your pint size. Your eyes are beautiful. And you tantalize a man with the austere glasses you wear. Take them off..."

He eased them from her face and carefully folded them, slipping them into her nerveless hand.

"With glasses you try to look like some old-fashioned girl. But with them off, however, you're one beautiful lady."

His head blotted out the sky as his mouth gently brushed against hers.

Molly closed her eyes and leaned into him, longing for more. He didn't fail her. His lips brushed again, then claimed hers in a kiss that was all-consuming. Tell's arms went around her and she was pulled to his warm chest.

Her glasses slipped from numb fingers and fell softly on the white sand as her hand moved against his skin, beneath his opened shirt, feeling the strong muscles ripple against her touch as she moved closer.

Her lips moved against his, the blood pounded in her heart, in her ears, through her body as his touch aroused her as never before. A hot, wild, searing kiss that went on and on.

For endless moments she felt beautiful.

One of the horses shoved against Molly, almost causing her to fall. She broke the kiss and stared up at Tell with wide, startled eyes, then turned to look at the horse.

Tell's eyes were a deep smoky gray as he gazed back down at her, taking in her tousled hair, her swollen lips.

"Four legged chaperones," he said whimsically.

Tell's face forcibly relaxed and he kissed her cheek, moving abruptly towards the horses, catching the reins and leading them near the edge of the beach where there was some vegetation.

"I'll tether the horses and we can go swimming."

Molly watched him lead the horses up the sand towards the sparse grass. She was glad to be able to plunge into the cool sea and hope it could quench the fire that burned deep in her for Tell Hardin.

She walked to the water's edge and hesitated. The waves looked bigger here than on Acapulco Bay beaches. The frothy water washed around her ankles. Dared she dive into the waves?

Tell joined her at water's edge.

"The surf here is strong; can you manage it?" Tell asked.

She nodded, afraid to trust her voice.

"Okay. Come on."

Taking her hand, he walked into the cool Pacific. Diving together through an incoming wave, they passed the crest and swam in the calm behind. The water was refreshing without being cold. The swells that lifted them then ran on past to crash against the beach added to the enjoyment. When she was tired, she lay on her back and floated. Tell swam near by, diving from time to time and staying down a long time. Molly wished she could hold her breath for as long.

"Ready to go back?" He was some yards away.

She rolled over to tread water. "Yes. Time for lunch?"

"I'm hungry, how about you?"

"Famished." She began swimming towards the shore.

In only a couple of strokes, Tell was beside her, lazily paddling alongside her as they moved with the swells.

"We can catch a wave and body-surf on in," he suggested.

"I'm willing to try, anyway," she replied, glancing over her shoulder to see the next swell.

Tell reached for her hand and strongly propelled them to the crest of the next wave. As it broke, they glided in on the frothy, churning white water, coming to a rest on the soft sand. Water drained from around them and Tell stood up, pulling Molly up before the next wave washed around them.

"That was fun," she exclaimed, happiness blooming again.

He watched her as she brushed some of the water off, slicked back her hair. For a moment, Molly thought he might kiss her again. But he said only, "Let's eat."

Tell provided an excellent lunch—cold fried chicken, chips, apples and cold drinks. The towel insulator had kept everything cool. They ate and watched the soothing rhythm of the surf, crashing over and over on the sandy bank, receding to crash again.

Molly became almost mesmerized by it, its soothing sound, regular beat and fascinating spray of colors a quiet beauty to lose oneself in. It would be so nice to always live by the beach.

"A penny for your thoughts." Tell broke into her dreaming.

"I was just thinking how perfect today is."

She turned to look at him, smiling at the picture he made. Brown and muscular, he lay on a towel, his head propped by one arm, his eyes closed. Molly remembered their first day at the beach in Acapulco. He was so very special. How could she bear it when they must part?

"So tell me more about Miss Molly Spencer," Tell invited drowsily.

Molly lay back on her towel, closing her eyes against the bright sun. The air was warm, a gentle breeze blew in from the water, and the only sound she could hear was the muffled surf.

"Like what?"

"How you happened on the kind of work you do, where you went to school, what you're going to do when you marry your rich husband."

"I never said I wanted to marry a rich man, only one who could offer security. My parents were dirt- poor. I'd never wish that on anyone."

"Did it ever occur to you that you might fall in love with someone who didn't have money? As your parents must have done?"

She was silent for a moment, fighting against the knowledge that refused to be hidden any longer.

She loved Tell Hardin.

She'd fallen for a man who had nothing—just like her mother.

But she wouldn't repeat her mother's mistake. She'd look for security.

If she could find it with love, so much the better. If not, security would be lasting.

"Did you fall asleep?" Tell asked.

"No, I... I won't fall for someone who's poor. I couldn't live like that all my life."

She couldn't bear the thought of raising children the way she'd been raised. She wanted more for her children.

"Money's not everything, Molly," he said easily.

"Maybe it's not for those who have it. But for me it represents the difference for everything. You're strong. You can make it doing whatever you want. And you're satisfied. But I don't want to live like I did before. Never knowing if I'd have a place to sleep. Food to eat. Clothes when I outgrew the clothes I wore."

"I think you're strong, talented. You have no reason to

depend on anyone else. You can make it on your own."

She rolled her head over to look at him. He was still lying back with his eyes closed, his chest rising and falling.

"I'm not strong," she whispered, looking away. "I'm so afraid sometimes."

"Well, everyone's afraid sometime," he said.

"Even you?"

He laughed, "Even me. What has your little mind invented for me—Superman?"

"No, but you never seem to care much for what others think. You seem so self- sufficient, so confident."

"I'm confident in myself and in things I do."

"Well, I'm not," she said.

"You should be. You've got talents, skills, experience. Be confident in that. You'll never be destitute. You'll be able to take care of yourself and anyone else who depends upon you. I don't know what your mother was like, but I'm beginning to know you."

Molly lay quiet. It was easy for him to say money didn't matter. He didn't suffer from feelings of inadequacy, fear of deprivation.

"Do you ride in rodeos?" she said, to change the subject.

She didn't want talk about her past any more. She thought all cowboys were in rodeos, and could easily imagine Tell on a bucking horse, taming him.

"Change of subject, huh? I used to. I'm too old now. I'm thirty-two. You need to be a young man to ride the rodeo circuit."

"Tell me about it," she invited.

And so he did. Told her about riding broncs in rodeos all over the west. Then segued into telling her about ranching in Texas. More stories of his brothers and sisters and cousins.

Molly loved listening to him talk. His voice was a pure

delight to listen to, his tales funny, heart-warming and so foreign to the girl who'd been alone most of her life.

When he asked more questions of her own life she slowly revealed some things she'd never thought she'd talk about.

And found the hurt she'd expected had eased—the memories weren't as painful as they once had been.

But her resolve remained strong. She'd never run the risk of any children of hers having a similar childhood.

It was a wonderful afternoon and she was sorry when he suggested they begin their ride back.

"It's not that late," she protested.

"But I want to take you on the dinner cruise on the bay tonight and you need to get back in time to shower and change for that," he said.

Her eyes lit up and her smile brightened her whole face.

She'd longed to go on the dinner cruise, never thinking she'd get the chance. And not with Tell.

For a moment, she paused. Was she to pay for the event as well?

Well, if so, so be it. She'd get her money's worth with the memories. Tomorrow she'd be back at work.

She pulled on the jeans and looked around for her shirt. Shaking out her towel, she rolled it up and stuffed it into her bag. She still didn't see her shirt.

Tell had his saddlebags tied on his horse and had donned his jeans. He wore no shirt and she watched him as he came up beside her leading the horses.

His skin was bronzed, his walk arrogant and cocky, his hat firmly on his head despite the afternoon breeze. He was gorgeous.

"Ready?" he asked.

"Almost. Have you seen my shirt?"

She should be looking for that, not at him.

"Yep."

"Where is it?"

"Packed away. I told you I didn't want you to wear a shirt."

She glanced down at her brief bikini-top, the snug jeans below.

"I can't ride home like this," she protested, thinking of all the people on the beach, those around the stables.

"Sure you can," he replied. "Why not?"

"Tell..."

"Come on, darlin", humor me."

She frowned, but knew arguing would prove futile.

Without another word, she struggled to get on her horse. Once seated, she gathered the reins and turned in the direction of the stables, urging her horse.

Cantering through the shallow waves, the water splashing up around her, Molly's frustration left and she laughed with the sheer pleasure of the day. Behind her she could hear the pounding of Tell's horse as he rode to overtake her.

She urged her mount faster, but Tell's horse was superior and he soon overtook her. Keeping the furious pace for several minutes, gradually they slowed. It was exhilarating.

When they reached the stables, the buildings were deserted. Tell led the horses inside and stripped them of their saddles, turning them out into the corral. Walking back into the dark interior of the stable, he saw Molly rummaging in his saddlebags, looking for her shirt.

"Uh-huh, I like you like you are."

He reached for the saddlebags.

She hung on, trying to find her shirt, laughing at his attempt to draw the saddlebags from her. He was teasing her, she knew it, because he could easily take them away if he wanted.

"I need my shirt."

"No." He pulled again, spinning her around the floor of the stable.

Molly laughed again. "Stop."

"Okay."

Lost to the sweet smell of hay, the dimness of the light, the heat of the afternoon, she could only feel Tell's mouth against hers. On and on the kiss went and Molly knew she was floating.

The day was hot, and so was the blood pounding through her body. His mouth was an endless source of sensuous excitement. When he moved to nibble at her earlobe, Molly almost sank to the ground, only his arms holding her kept her upright.

"Pardon, senor"

The gentle Spanish voice broke the spell. Tell stepped back slowly and tapped her lips with his finger. His eyes were smoky as he stared at her swollen lips, his finger tracing lightly.

"Sorry, senior. Thank you for returning the horses. They were good?" the man asked.

"They were fine."

With a sigh, Tell straightened completely. Molly moved on shaky legs out into the bright sun as Tell crossed the stable to talk to the man. Slowly she walked to the car, thoughts of her shirt forgotten.

Her heart pounded at the kisses they'd shared.

She loved Tell, ached with longing for him, but dared not let him know.

How he'd laugh.

First because he wasn't well established, as she'd said a man would need to be, and second because he'd never given her any indication he wanted anything more than a holiday fling, someone to pass the time with while he vacationed in Acapulco.

It'd all end soon.

This was a fairy-tale, not real.

And when it ended, as it had to, he'd go back to Texas and she'd go back to LA. Their lives were too different.

Sadness welled up where happiness had been.

Tell joined her in the car and drove to the hotel.

"I'll pick you up at seven-thirty. The cruise starts at eight. Wear that pretty dress you had on the other night."

Molly looked over at him, a hint of a smile in her glance. The magic wasn't over yet. There was still tonight and all the tomorrows that he was here. She'd store the memories to treasure down the years ahead.

Smiling at him, she nodded, glad he'd see her in the pretty dress one more time.

When they pulled up before Molly's casita, they saw the blue and white jeep parked before it. Beverley was back.

Molly's heart sank. Was this the end to the night's plans? Could she still go or would Beverley be ready to work again?

Molly was afraid to find out. She wanted to go on the cruise more than anything right now.

Tell stopped the car and reached in the back for her tote. Walking around the car to open her door, he glanced at the jeep.

"Boss back?"

"Looks like it. I don't know if this'll change things."

"It won't. If she asks you to do anything, tell her you'll have to do it in the morning—you have plans tonight. She won't expect you to change them."

"Maybe."

Molly wasn't convinced.

If she were going with Luis, Beverley would be delighted. But Molly had been warned against Tell.

"I'll be here at seven-thirty."

He kissed her cheek and slammed the door, watching as Molly walked away.

She paused at the door, and smiled boldly. "I'll be ready."

Ten

Molly let herself into her room quietly. If Beverley was sleeping or busy writing, Molly didn't want to alert her that she was home. She moved to the sliding glass door and looked out. No sign of Beverley on the patio. No noise coming from her room.

Closing the curtains, Molly began to get ready for the evening ahead.

Stepping beneath the warm shower, feeling the soothing water wash away the salt and sand from the day's outing, Molly let herself remember Tell's kisses. The feel of his mouth against hers, against her breast. The rapture she felt in his arms. Then she remembered the kisses from the other night.

Had Beverley not interrupted, where would she be today? Would she know the full love in her heart was shared by him?

Or was she only a conquest during the vacation, forgotten once she'd gone?

Drying off, she determined that she'd enjoy the evening and not think of the future, not consider what might have been. She knew where she was headed and could not, dare not, deviate from her chosen plan.

To do so would court disaster such as her mother had faced.

Knowing that, she could still spend time with Tell, enjoy

herself, as long as she knew it wouldn't last. She could manage that much.

It'd been inevitable once she'd turned on the shower that Beverley knew she was back. Soon after she donned her dress, she heard the soft tap at her sliding glass door. Drawing open the curtains, Molly opened the door.

"Hello, dear. Back, I see. Oh, you're dressed up. Going out?"

"Yes. I've been invited to the dinner cruise. Did you need me?"

Molly held her breath. Please don't let anything spoil the night. She hadn't realized how much she was looking forward to the evening until she considered it might be canceled. She longed to feel Tell's arms about her as they danced, to feel the length of his body against hers as they swayed to music. She wanted just this one night, and prayed that nothing would spoil it.

"Oh, no. You go on and have a good time. You look very nice. I didn't realize Luis was back. Did you enjoy your days off? I had such fun in Taxco, bought more silver than I should have, but I do love shopping there. Come by later and I'll show you all my treasures. Maybe Luis would like to see them, too?"

Before Molly could answer, Beverley patted her on the arm.

"Don't let me keep you. I know you want to look your best. Just pop by if you have time later. If not, tomorrow will do. I feel energized again. Think I'll dictate some tapes tonight. We'll be going full blast tomorrow. Have fun."

Beverley smiled and strolled out to the patio, walking near the railing.

Molly breathed a sigh of relief as she slid her door closed and turned to apply her make-up. The tan from the tropical sun gave her all the color she needed. A touch of mascara and she was ready.

She was ready long before seven-thirty. Each minute dragged by endlessly. She longed for him to arrive, yet dreaded the possibility of a confrontation between him and her employer. Beverley was still on the patio. With luck, when Tell arrived, Molly could slip out and Beverley would never see who her escort for the evening was.

Hearing the sound of his car, Molly grabbed her bag and let herself quietly out of the room. She quickly walked down the short walkway to the drive, anxious to get in the car and get away.

Tell arose on the far side of the car. He was dressed in tan trousers, a white shirt and navy blazer. Molly wondered where he'd come up with the clothes. She'd only seen him in cut-offs and jeans. He looked decidedly handsome. She really didn't care, was glad to see him.

"You look nice," she blurted out, her heart swelling in anticipation of the evening ahead.

He smiled and came around the car.

"So do you."

He skimmed the back of his fingers down her arm as if he had to touch her.

He held the door open for her and shut it carefully, as if she was precious cargo. For a wild, rough cowboy, he sure knew how to make her feel special.

Throwing a quick glance over her shoulder as they pulled away, Molly was reassured she saw no sign of Beverley as they drove away. Breathing a sigh of relief, she turned back to the front.

"And what was that for?" Tell asked.

"What?"

"What? That sigh."

"Oh, nothing. I'm glad we're going, that's all," she told him.

"No trouble with your boss?"

"No."

"Did she know you were going out?"

"Yes."

Tell sighed and pulled to the side of the narrow road.

"What's up?" His narrow gaze pinned her to the seat of the car.

She fidgeted beneath his gaze and looked away.

"Nothing."

"Something's up," he commanded.

"Not really. Beverley thinks I'm going out with Luis Alverado."

"Ashamed to be out with me, Molly?"

His voice was silky, but the instant anger could not be completely covered.

She faced him. "No, of course not. I wouldn't ever want you to think that. It's just that Beverley told me that first day in Acapulco to stay away from you and I don't want to jeopardize my job. I told you that before."

"She wouldn't fire you for seeing me."

"I don't want to take the chance."

"So you'd rather lie?"

"No, I didn't lie. She thinks it's Luis, I just didn't correct her."

"I must remember you're not so above board when it suits you not to be." His voice was still grim.

"Don't be mad. I wanted this evening to be perfect."

He turned to the front again, his hands gripping the wheel hard.

For a moment, Molly wondered why he should be so angry. She was not ashamed to be seen with him, only trying to keep away from a confrontation with her boss.

"Before I forget."

His voice was cold. He reached into his pocket and drew

out several folded notes, handing them to Molly. "I really only wanted a loan today. I forgot my wallet, though I know you thought I was cadging off you."

She stared at the money, a feeling of guilt and shame invading. She had thought that.

Why hadn't she trusted him? Why couldn't she let go of the past and judge people on what they seemed? Why blame him for her father's lack?

"Thank you," she said softly, taking for the money.

No wonder he was mad at her—all her actions seemed to point out that she was ashamed of him. And she wasn't.

She enjoyed being with him. It made her happy and proud to be seen with him. How could she convey this to him?

She tucked the money in her purse as he put the car in gear and started up again. The ride was silent. Neither spoke as he negotiated the curves and hills leading down to Acapulco.

Molly was miserable.

She'd so looked forward to their evening together. Now it was spoiled because of her.

She should have believed him earlier, believed in him, that it was only a loan. She should have stood up to Beverley and told her about Tell.

She was her own person—surely she was entitled to see whomever she liked in her free time.

Tell was right. It was highly unlikely she'd be fired for dating someone Beverley didn't like. Beverley was engrossed in her work. She had nothing to do with Molly's choice in companions.

Darting a quick glance at Tell, she felt disappointed and frustrated. She didn't want the evening to continue like this.

It'd be better to call it off.

"Tell."

She reached out her hand to touch him, resting it on his

thigh. Instantly, his hand came to cover hers, resting on the warm muscles of his leg, his fingers tightening on hers. She caught her breath at the surge of emotion that engulfed her at his touch.

"Sometimes I could wring your neck, Molly Spencer. I can't figure you out. I think you like my company and then you insult me. You seek me out with Miguel and deny me to your boss. You make me so angry. Yet you also smile when you see me. You kiss like no one I've ever kissed. Sometimes I think you like me–until the next insult."

"I'm sorry. I do want to spend time with you, I like spending time with you. I'm sorry I didn't let Beverley know it was you I'm going out with. Don't be mad. I want to enjoy tonight. I enjoy being with you."

He sighed and squeezed her hand again. He said nothing, but the tension between them seemed to gradually fade away.

Parking the car near the docks, Tell threaded her fingers through his as he led the way to the sparkling white ship that cruised Acapulco Bay and short stretches into the Pacific. Across an expanse of water was the dock of one of the luxury liners that stopped in Acapulco, its gleaming white sides towering over the dock, its lights illuminating the entire waterway. Festive, colorful flags fluttered in the evening breeze. There was an excitement in the air that was infectious.

Molly's spirits rose despite the rocky start.

Boarding the dinner ship, Molly was enchanted. It had a large dining area, its windows opened to the soft, scented air. Before and aft were large decks, small tables and chairs lining the rails. The open space obviously for dancing.

Following the steward, Molly entered the dining- room and soon was seated at a table beside one of the large, open windows. The dining-room was full without being crowded. There was a small bar at one end. Despite the other people,

Molly felt she and Tell were in a world of their own.

"This is perfect," she said as she looked out of the window when they pulled away from the dock at the lights sparkling along the beaches of Acapulco.

The water was calm reflecting the lights from the rows of hotels lining the shore as dusk turned into night. Here and there in the large bay she saw the running lights of smaller boats, their owners also out to enjoy an evening on the water.

"I took the liberty of ordering for us earlier—I suppose you want to argue about that," Tell said whimsically.

She looked at him and smiled. "No, I don't. It sounds fine to me."

He raised one eyebrow in mock astonishment and Molly felt her heart crash against her chest.

Oh, heavens, if just looking at him caused this reaction, what would dancing with him do? She swallowed hard and looked back out of the window. Maybe coming here had been a mistake after all. Yet she could hardly wait.

As the ship pulled away from the harbor the stewards began serving dinner. The soft strains from the band floated in through the open windows. The song they played forever etched itself in Molly's memory as a part of Mexico.

The steward placed their plates before them. The medallions of veal and the fresh asparagus were delicious. Molly complimented Tell on his choice. She'd make a special effort to make him feel as special as he made her feel.

She wanted him to always remember her as special.

From then on they regained their former ease. Talking casually about the cruise, the sights from the ship, Tell pointed out Las Casitas D'Oro high on the distant hillside. The ship glided west, out to sea, then turned north to run along the coast for an hour or two before returning to port.

When they finished eating, Tell asked her to dance. Molly

nodded, anticipation and anxiety warring. She longed to be in his arms again, but wondered if she could keep her secret safe.

One touch from him set her emotions in a spin—could she dance with him all evening, be wrapped in his arms and not blurt out her love for him? Could she stand the gentle torment of touching him and not letting him know how much she cared?

Tell led her to the aft deck. It was darker than the one on the bow and less crowded. Sheltered from the breeze somewhat by the structure of the dining-room, it was warm and intimate. He drew her into his arms and began to move with the soft music.

His legs brushed against hers and sent shock waves of delight and yearning coursing through her body. His arms held her tightly against him. She could feel his heartbeat match her own.

Molly encircled his neck with her arms, pressing against his chest, moving her hips and legs as he led. The two of them moved as one to the haunting melody.

One of his hands splayed against the bare skin of her back, holding her firmly against him. The other rested on her hips and moved as she moved, its heat penetrating the light material of her dress. Molly grew warmer. Perhaps they should be on the front deck; she needed the extra breeze to cool down.

Seduced by his touch, the romantic music and the floating euphoria of the cruise, she reached up and pulled his head down to her mouth. She wanted to feel his kiss, to dance in time with the dreamy music, lost in the rhapsody of Tell's body against hers, the feel of his lips and mouth on hers adding to the measure of fantasy she felt.

His hands moved until they were on either side of her hips, moving her against him from side to side, slowly, sensuously.

His mouth left hers to trail hot kisses along her cheek, her jaw, down her neck to the pulsating spot on her throat, back to her mouth.

Molly's legs were weak and trembling. She clung to Tell in a mist of desire and yearning. Her body clamored for his and she was impatient with the constraints between them and the limitations of the boat.

He broke off, and pulled her to the side, sitting in one of the chairs in the shadow of the engine-room.

"Much more of this and I'll ask the captain for a room. I want to talk to you."

His voice was ragged, his breathing erratic.

"Mmm."

She kissed him again, snuggling up against his strong chest, feeling his hands on her waist, caressing her through the flimsy soft material of her dress.

"Molly, I'm leaving. I'm going back to Texas. My vacation is over."

The words hit her like cold water.

The feeling of euphoria and happiness vanished instantly.

Her voice was thick, and she could scarcely get the words out.

"Leaving?" She knew it'd come. She'd known it all along. But so soon?

"Yes. I do work, you know. Even though you think I'm some sort of bum. I have to get back." He looked at her for a long moment. "Come with me."

She sat up, pushing away from him. She was too disorientated to stand just yet.

Trying to breathe, to feel something beside the aching pain in her heart, she let his words echo over and over. Was her world ending?

Trying to keep it light, she painted a smile on her face and faced him, but couldn't quite meet his eyes.

"To your bunkhouse? You never did say if it'd be just the two of us."

"I'm serious, Molly."

"Me, too. I can't go with you."

There, she'd said it.

Was that pain in her chest her heart breaking? She took a deep breath, trying to free the coldness that was pressing down on her.

"Trust me, Molly. Trust me to care for you, look after you. Come with me."

No words of love. Had he learned nothing about her these weeks.

It was daring to share a vacation together, something quite different to go off to Texas together.

What did he want? To continue their holiday romance? She knew he wanted her; every action he'd ever done had proved that. Was it the quest of the chase, satisfied when won?

"I can't go with you."

She stood up, moving to the railing. The night felt cold, or was it only her? She wished she'd brought a sweater.

He followed, swinging her round to face him.

"Why not? Because of money? If I were some rich guy you'd come in an instant, wouldn't you? Women will do anything for money. Can't you trust me, Molly? Trust me to never let you be in want? Come with me, as we are, and take a chance on the future."

Sadly she shook her head, too afraid to take what he offered, too sure she knew where it'd all lead–down a path she'd been as a child and didn't care to go again.

"I can't come with you. But thank you for asking me. I'll always treasure that."

For heaven's sake, she sounded like some eighteenth century young girl.

Her voice broke on the last part and she turned away, blinking her eyes furiously. She refused to cry. She'd known all along there was no future for them.

She thought she'd have more time in Acapulco.

For a long moment he said nothing, then in a strained voice he said softly, "I'll miss you, darlin'."

It was almost more than she could stand.

"Could we dance again?" she asked, her voice tinged with sadness.

He drew her into his arms and moved back to the floor, swaying to the music, moving in time, but more like strangers, no longer close like before.

Molly felt encased in ice. She was numb to all feelings, except for where her body touched his. There she burned.

He was leaving and she was staying. Their wonderful meetings would end. No longer would she feel delightfully daring doing something not quite proper. No longer be able to look forward to seeing him, learning something new, something different, as she had all along with this arrogant, forceful, exciting cowboy.

The cruise became an endless nightmare. Molly wanted it to end, her anticipation of earlier only a cruel reminder of how much she'd looked forward to the evening. Now she wanted to get off the boat, away from Tell, escape to the sanctuary of her own room. Had time stopped?

They danced, watched the shore as the boat returned to the bay, and disembarked with the others from the ship, the other people who'd had a wonderful time, who were laughing and happy. Molly felt as if she were in a trance, soon to end. She hoped.

She said nothing as Tell whisked them through the city, up the hillside to her hotel. Pulling up before her door, he turned off the engine but made no moves beyond that.

Molly didn't want to move. To do so would end the evening, end her time with Tell forever. Yet it was already over. All over. Everything had changed.

He touched her lips gently with his finger. "I want you, Molly. If you change your mind, leave a message with Miguel."

"Goodnight, Tell." She couldn't bring herself to say goodbye.

She yanked open her door and fled the car, not wanting him to touch her again lest she lose all control and give in to the longings of her heart.

Gaining the safety of her room, she leaned against her door, listening for the sound of the car, hearing it start, pull away.

He was gone.

Molly burst into tears.

It was her own fault. She'd been playing with fire since that first night on the terrace. She never should have gone along with him. But he brought such excitement and novelty to her life. She was tired of the regimented life she'd set for herself. It had been such fun to do the unexpected with Tell.

He'd made her feel so alive, so daring. From buying that scandalous bikini, to their rainy rendezvous at supper at his camp, to the wild ride along the beach, he'd had her do things she'd never thought of before. Fun things, exciting out of the ordinary things.

Fairy-tale kind of excitement.

She dressed for bed, and climbed under the sheets, tears flowing steadily. Curling up in a ball, she tried to ease the ache in her heart, the loneliness that felt so overwhelming. Nothing worked. Crying softly in the night, Molly finally fell asleep.

She awoke the next morning with a raging headache. Donning her swimsuit, she went for a quick dip in the pool, the cool water refreshing, the invigorating exercise a balm to her battered nerves.

She felt better for the swim and was able to greet Beverley pleasantly a short time later when they met for breakfast.

"Tell me about Taxco," Molly urged, hoping to start her employer on a monologue so she'd have little need to contribute to the conversation.

"It was wonderful. I went to the shops that actually beat the silver into thin strips before making the most exquisite jewelry."

Beverley launched into the details of her trip, capturing the nuances of the old city so well that Molly felt as if she'd seen it in person. She listened to Beverley, focusing her attention on her every word to avoid thinking about Tell.

"Goodness, look at the time. I wanted to get an early start today." Beverley glanced at her watch. "And you haven't even told me how your days off were. How was the cruise?"

"Very nice." Molly rose and moved around the pool, not wanting to talk about anything, but especially not last night. "I'll get the computer turned on and collect the tape you did last night," she said.

Throwing herself into her work, Molly sought to forget by sheer determination. She transcribed each tape almost as soon as Beverley drew it from the recorder.

Reviewing her transcriptions each night, she corrected any typos and misspellings. Staying up late until fatigue overcame her and she stumbled to bed was the only way she could get any sleep.

Despite her efforts, thoughts of Tell crept in.

When was he leaving?

Would he come by to see her one more time before going? Or was he waiting for some word from her before coming again? Should she send him a message from Miguel? Yet what could she say? Only goodbye.

Over and over she tried to imagine his life, working on a ranch, repairing fences, branding cattle. What else did he do?

What did he do in the evenings? Would he work late to avoid thinking of her? Or sit on a wooden porch and watch the evening come over the plains, sit with other cowboys and swap stories? Would he think of her or would her memory fade after a few weeks?

She wished she could have gone with him, if only for a visit.

Maybe seeing him in his setting would resolve things for her. At least she'd know in the future what kind of life he led, what his home looked like, what he did in his spare time.

Now she'd always wonder.

It made her heart ache.

Molly endured it for two days.

The third morning when she awoke she resolved to send Tell a message. Miguel could get word to him. She'd see him once more. Maybe she explore the possibility of coming to visit.

But of course, since she was in a hurry, Beverley was particularly demanding that morning. She wanted to verify several items she'd already incorporated in the book, forcing Molly to find the passages and read them back to her.

After editing over and over, at last she was satisfied.

"That's all for today. I think I'll go to the beach club later. Want to ride down with me?" she asked.

"I may."

Molly first wanted to get a message to Tell. Would he come this afternoon? Should she hang around in case he did? How soon was he leaving?

She longed to see him again, had to see him one more time.

She hurried down to the lobby. Miguel's quiet smile greeted her when she entered the breezy expanse.

"Buenos dias, senorita."

"Hello, Miguel. I want to send a message to Senor Hardin."

His face fell. "But senorita, Senor Hardin, he is gone. His holidays ended and he is gone back to Texas."

"I didn't know," she said, her hopes sinking.

He'd waited until the last moment to tell her he was leaving.

He hadn't given her any time to come to terms with his departure.

So, after all, he'd gone. Without a word of farewell, without seeing her again. Leave word with Miguel, he'd said. What for? So the next time he was down this way he'd learn that she'd changed her mind?

When would he ever come to Acapulco again? Would she?

She walked listlessly back up the steep hill to the casita.

"Goodbye, Tell," she said softly as the tears started again.

Eleven

Time crept by. Molly no longer enjoyed the simple things that'd brought her pleasure before. Everything reminded her of Tell.

From the beauty of the view from her patio to swimming at the beach club, everything she did held memories.

Was there a place in Acapulco she didn't associate with Tell?

Only the house of Luis Alverado. And she had no interest in renewing acquaintance with that nice young man when he'd called to say he was back in town and wanted to see her.

She'd rather do her job, then go for the long walks that had been her solace in the last few days.

She'd once wondered if she'd ever tire of the view from her room and she hadn't. But it caused her more pain than delight now.

She remembered the first night she'd seen the stranger lurking in the shadows, how he'd frightened her at first, then intrigued her. He'd pointed out the hotels across the bay and told her about the cruise ships.

Molly stood by the railing, looking out over the sunset, the sky vibrant shades of pink, mauve and purple. In the distance she saw one of the bright luxury cruise ships and she could almost hear the music from it.

"Trust me, Molly. Trust me to care for you".

The words Tell had spoken echoed in her mind. She wished she could trust him. While he was young and fit now, what would the years bring? Would he be killed young, like her father? Leaving her and a child, or, worse, children, to fend for themselves.

"You're strong", he'd said.

She didn't feel strong. She felt afraid again.

Afraid she'd lost something invaluable, yet afraid to trust someone as carefree as Tell. She needed stability and security in her life. She couldn't afford to gamble.

Slowly the words held more meaning. She'd brought herself up from poverty to a nice standard of living.

So maybe her fate wasn't that of her mother's.

Maybe she could love a man, work with him to build a life together, one they'd share until both were old. Maybe he wouldn't die young and leave her destitute.

"You've got talents, skills... you'd never be destitute..."

She could get an office job anywhere. Good clerical help was always in demand. She was a hard worker and good at her skills.

Beverley had complimented her several times, and she was a hard taskmaster.

Trust me. Trust me. Trust me.

The words echoed over and over in her mind.

Molly's eyes no longer saw the sunset and its glorious colors; she saw only Tell's dark face. She heard his voice, low and compelling, urging her to trust him, depend on him, count on him. He wouldn't let her down.

Could she do it? Could she throw all her plans out the window and follow the cowboy who'd captured her heart?

What was the alternative? Endless years of the loneliness this last week had given her? Longing for the man she loved, wanting to be with him, wanting him to be with her?

She'd made a mistake in saying no. Could she correct it?

She loved him. She had to accept that.

Could she trust him?

Her heart wouldn't let her do otherwise.

The decision made, a great sense of peace invaded her.

She needed to talk to Tell, to let him know she'd changed her mind, that she couldn't go on without him. She loved him, she wanted to be with him. Why did he have to be so far away when she made the most important discovery of her life?

Slowly she walked back to her room. If she couldn't talk to him, maybe Miguel knew where she could mail a letter. She'd write to him, to see if he felt the same about wanting her to come to Texas.

And if he didn't?

The thought didn't bear thinking about.

Dear Tell. I'll come. I miss you too much to stay away. Trust me, you said. I do. I trust you with my life, my future, my heart. I love you. If you still want me to come to Texas, please let me know where. Love, Molly.

She re-read it. Was it too forward?

She smiled, imagining his teasing her about being so focused on security. This was as wildly opposite to stability as possible for her. However daring, it was the only thing that might bring her happiness.

She put the letter in an envelope and walked down to the lobby. It was late, and the night clerk behind the desk told her Miguel was off duty and wouldn't be back until the morning. Could he help?

Reluctantly, Molly explained that she wanted an address from Miguel. The clerk took the envelope and wrote a note, leaving both on the desk for Miguel when he arrived the next morning.

"It will be taken care of, senorita." He smiled at her, not at all struck by the oddness of the request.

Molly's heart felt lighter as she went to bed that night. Soon Tell would get the letter, soon she'd hear from him. She just had to.

Miguel called her the next morning.

"Senorita, I have your letter to Senor Hardin. I do not know if the address I have for him is any good. It was one given long ago. He may have moved."

Molly's spirits dropped. She'd so counted on Miguel knowing how to contact him.

"Send it to the address you have. If he's moved, perhaps they'll forward it. Thank you, Miguel."

She hung up. Now it was only a matter of time. Time and luck that the address was correct.

The work on the book was drawing to an close. Molly could tell from the events taking place that General Pershing was drawing near the end of his career.

Beverley dictated tirelessly, and Molly's fingers flew to keep up with the tapes. With the end in sight, there was all the more reason to keep on.

Beverley walked in very solemnly one morning and stood beside Molly. Dramatically she handed the tape to her secretary.

"The last one," she said.

"Already? It's gone by so fast," Molly murmured, taking the tape.

"Yes, but I had it mapped out before the actual dictating. I knew as I was doing the research how I'd tell his life. And this is only the first draft. We still have weeks of work left. But I'm glad this is over. I feel drained."

Beverley wandered out to the patio.

Molly inserted the tape into the machine. Now she'd see the final scenes of Black Jack's life, and the wrap-up that Beverley was known for.

There was still editing and re-writes to be done, but the major effort of the book was complete. Molly felt excited. The re-writes and polishing was still ahead, but she'd at least know the ending.

She finished the last page before dinner.

Beverley was sitting on the patio, gazing out over the bay, a stiff drink in her hand.

"I'm done. It's wonderful, Beverley."

Molly plopped in the chair beside her, her praise honest.

"Thank you. We'll leave in the morning," Beverley said, smiling at her secretary.

"Leave? For where?"

"Home. I got a call from my sister. She figured I should be about finished now and wants me to stop by before returning to LA. I told her we'd leave in the morning, stay a few days with her then return to LA. There's still lots to do on this book before I can submit it, but the next part is the grinding part. We'll take a few days at her place, then lock ourselves up in my place at Malibu and work day and night until it's done."

"But. I guess I thought we'd stay here a little longer."

Panic touched Molly. Tell didn't know where she lived.

If she left here, how would he reach her?

She'd been hoping daily for some word from him. She couldn't just disappear.

Quickly her mind sorted through ideas. She'd have to send him another letter, letting him know of the change of plans, giving him her cell phone number. The phone would work again once she was back in the States.

If she'd only suspected Beverley planned to leave so precipitately she'd have included it in her letter.

It'd been a week. She didn't even know if he'd received her letter. Had he changed his mind? Or was his letter to her even now on its way back?

"No need to stay. I've finished the book, you've finished the tapes, pack up tonight. Tomorrow we leave on the ten am. flight. Where shall we go for our last night in Acapulco?"

Molly must have given an answer because Beverley rose to get dressed, but she didn't remember speaking. Her thoughts were whirling.

She'd have to write to Tell immediately and wished she knew where to reach him. Wished she'd still be in Acapulco when he contacted her.

Now she'd have to wait weeks or so before she could possibly hear from him. She'd send a letter with her home address and phone number. And hope the address Miguel had was still valid.

Did cowboys drift to different ranches?

Blast. Each day seemed like an eternity. It could be weeks before she'd get his answer.

She wanted to hear from him now.

If he'd had a computer, she could have gotten his email address. Or a phone number? Would it have been too much for him to give her a phone number?

Beverley and Molly ate at one of the seaside restaurants on the beach. The scampi was delicious, but Molly scarcely tasted it.

She sat absorbing every last sight she could of Acapulco. It was her last night in this magical paradise and she wanted to remember it.

Whatever happened, Acapulco was the place where she'd fallen in love.

She remembered Tell's last night, and wished she'd found the courage to accept him when he'd asked her to come away. Wished she could have seen him once more before he left. Wished she'd been brave enough to agree to go with him then, though she'd have needed to stay through the end of the book.

She owed Beverley that much.

She packed quickly when they reached their rooms. Then she hastily drafted another letter to Tell. In the morning she'd leave it with Miguel. He'd mail it for her and Tell could be calling her by the time they reached LA. She'd

forgotten to ask Beverley where her sister lived—if it was Southern California, maybe Molly needn't stay there and could be home by supper.

They stopped at the desk the next morning to drop off their keys and turn in the gaily colored blue and white jeep. A taxi was taking them to the airport. Molly took the opportunity to look for Miguel. He wasn't on duty, Carlos was.

Molly's heart sank.

"Is Miguel coming in today?" she asked, glancing over her shoulder to make sure she wasn't holding Beverley up.

"No, senorita, it is his day off. He will return in two days. Can I help you?"

"Do you know Senor Hardin?"

"No, I do not believe I know the senor. Is he registered here?"

"No. I... he's not even in Mexico any more. He lives in Texas. Miguel knows where. I wanted to send him a letter."

"I'm sorry, senorita, I do not know him."

"Could I leave the letter for Miguel to send?"

"Si, I will tell him."

Dissatisfied with the way things were going, Molly had no choice but to hand over the envelope, with a few pesos for postage. She smiled her thanks and hurried to join Beverley as the taxi pulled up.

Down the Carretera Escenica, Acapulco Bay behind them. Soon they crested the last hill and dropped down the other side, the sight of the beautiful city lost from view.

Along this road Molly and Tell had driven to reach the

Revolcadero Beach, to ride the horses.

Her eyes filled with tears. She'd been so happy that day. Until his announcement that night shattered her serenity. Despite her accusations and suspicions, he'd wanted her to come with him.

She wished she'd said yes.

Past the turn-off, the beautiful Acapulco Princess, the pyramid hotel rising from the beach on their right. On the taxi sped, to the airport.

Molly gazed at the scene with sadness.

Would her letters reach Tell? Would he want to see her after she'd so adamantly refused him when he'd first asked her to come with him?

What if he didn't want her any more? What if it had just been a vacation fling, a fun memory of his time in Mexico? How would she stand that?

She was numb when they reached the airport. She stood by while the cab driver unloaded their bags. Taking the laptop, she watched as the other bags were checked in.

"Where does your sister live?" she asked Beverley as that lady headed into the terminal.

"We're flying into Dallas, then we'll get a connecting flight to Laredo. We'll be met there, driven to the ranch," Beverley said as she headed toward the security lines.

"Ranch?" Molly said.

Texas? Tell lived in Texas.

"Mmm, Sally lives on a ranch. I come from that area. Raised there. Tell will probably pick us up. He lives closest to the airport."

"Tell Harden?"

A strange confusion exploded. She felt as if she were near a momentous discovery, her heartbeat sped up. She turned to stare at Beverley.

"Yes. You met him in Acapulco one day," Beverley said, pulling the airline tickets from her purse.

"Yes, you—er—warned me away from him, I thought."

Molly was trying to make sense of this. "Do you know him?"

"Honey, I've known him all his life—he's my nephew, Sally's oldest boy."

Molly was thunderstruck. She stared at Beverley, almost unable to believe her ears, her mind scrambling to make sense of this totally unexpected revelation.

"Tell Hardin's your nephew. But you told me he was nothing but trouble."

"Oh, he's that, all right. Trouble for any pretty young girl. He likes girls. They like him, too much I think. He's always fending them off. But he's a hot-headed, wild kid. Comes from having so much money, spending it, being sought after for his money, I guess. He doesn't cotton to any kind of commitment or long- term relationship. Twice I've thought he was close, but the girls just wanted the money. He's been burned so badly I doubt he'll ever marry. You're too nice to be taken in by Tell. That's why I warned you away. You're too naive for the likes of him. He's a hell raiser from way back. He'd be nothing but trouble for someone like you."

Tell had thought her too conservative. He'd often teased her about it. Yet he'd asked her to come away with him.

But the most startling fact was his aunt was telling her he had money.

"He has money?"

Why hadn't he told her? Had he just been toying with her, as Beverley suggested? He knew security was important to her. Why hadn't he told her?

"Sure, though you'd never guess from the way he carries on in Mexico. He likes to camp rather than stay in one of the hotels, dresses like a beach bum and goes to cheap restaurants. Says it's his way to get with real people again. I'd like to know what he thinks his family is made of—fake people? Jim, that's their dad, he gave the kids each some cash to start off with. Tell's done well with his share, bought a ranch, makes money at it, too."

"So he owns the ranch, doesn't just work there," Molly said, almost to herself.

"He works darn hard. But he also has a strong ties with his family. That's why he was down in Acapulco, looking out for me. Sally told him I was coming here and so he dropped by to make sure I was doing okay. Really, my family acts as if I can't get along myself. Anyway, I only saw him once. He must have gone home after that."

No, he hadn't, Molly sighed softly.

But it might have been better if he had.

"I don't know why Sally wants me to stop by, but she rarely asks for anything, so I might as well visit her. We'll just delay polishing the book for a few days. You'll like their place, out in the hills, beautiful country, not a bit like LA. Though I like LA. I couldn't wait to leave Texas when I went to college. It'll always be home, but give me LA every time."

When their flight was called, they boarded in first class. Molly had the window seat. She made sure Beverley was settled, then turned to look out at the bustling activity on the tarmac her thoughts spinning.

She could scarcely take it all in. It was the furthest thing from her mind when she left the hotel. She'd been so distraught to be leaving before contacting Tell. Now it looked as if she would be seeing him in a few hours.

Trust me, he'd said.

She smiled; she had trusted in him. She'd decided to follow him before she knew who he was, before she knew he could offer her the security and stability she craved. She'd trusted her heart before she knew.

Her heart beat faster and a loving smile touched her face, grew. She'd be seeing him soon. She'd be able to tell him in person how much she loved him.

Had he been glad when he read her letter? Was it really his mother who'd arranged their visit or Tell through his mother?

Molly could hardly wait to see him again. The depression of the last few days vanished instantly.

They changed planes in Dallas and Molly took the time to make sure her make-up was fresh and her hair combed. Excited about the upcoming meeting, she was impatient with the delay but tried to hide it from Beverley. She wore the suit she'd traveled to Mexico in, the one Tell had seen her in the first night on the patio. Would he remember it? She wished she could have worn one of her new blouses and a pair of shorts, but this was more appropriate for travel.

The short flight from Dallas to Laredo was soon over, and Molly and Beverley entered the air-conditioned airport building. Scanning the waiting crowd, Molly's heart sped up when she spotted Tell's tall figure, standing a bit behind the others, tall and arrogant. Wearing his hat, she could still see his eyes when he saw her. His eyes clashed with hers.

She smiled and waved, happiness bubbling up, love shining from her face.

His glance was enigmatic, his expression non-committal. He didn't smile back, his eyes narrowed and he looked as if he was considering what to say.

Her heart skipped a beat. He looked wonderful. She was so glad to see him again.

He was as tall as ever, dressed in tight jeans and a blue and white checked shirt. He wore cowboy boots and hat. Molly feasted her eyes on him, her own love shining out.

"Hello, Tell," she said shyly as they approached.

He nodded, leaning over to kiss his aunt on her cheek.

"Hello, Beverley, Molly."

"Well, what does your mother need that I have to come all the way over here for a visit? Couldn't she come visit me in LA?" Beverley asked, looking up at her tall nephew.

"You'll have to ask her. I just came to pick you up."

His eyes never left Molly's. But he didn't seem happy to see her. Not the way she felt–over the top with happiness.

She wondered if they would get to have some privacy soon. Maybe he didn't want to speak before his aunt.

He must have received her letter by now. Had she been too bold or totally misread the situation? Doubts crowded her mind. Had he changed his mind? Had it been only the wine and the moonlight talking? Had it only been a holiday fling, one he didn't want known by his family?

"Ready?"

Molly nodded and moved to Beverley's far side. She didn't understand. Why didn't Tell seem happier to see her? He'd asked her to come away with him. Had he changed his mind?

Maybe it was one thing for her to flit off with him, but something else to arrive with his aunt.

Didn't he want his family to know about her? Uncertainty began to build.

She wished now that she hadn't come with Beverley. She should have insisted she return home to wait for Beverley there.

How awkward it would be if he didn't want her anymore. Color washed in her face, as she avoided looking at him.

Molly and Beverley had to walk quickly through the airport to keep up with Tell's longer stride. He fetched their luggage and soon had it stowed in his large pick-up truck.

"You sit in the middle, Molly, I want the window." Beverley paused at the door.

Tell's lips tightened, but he said nothing as Molly slid across the seat. After closing the door behind Beverley, he went around and climbed in.

His leg was only inches from Molly's and she could feel the heat radiating from it in the hot afternoon. His arm brushed hers as he turned the wheel. She pulled slightly away, puzzled by his reaction, her arm tingling at his touch. Was he mad?

"How are your folks?" Beverley asked as they reached the highway.

"Doing well. Diane's home with the baby. Ellie will be over on the weekend. How long are you staying?" Tell asked, ignoring Molly.

"I don't know. It depends on your mother. I've finished the draft of the book, might as well take a few days off before starting in on the editing stage. You know I like to do all that at one stretch. We'll return to LA for that. I'll be glad to see the baby, I bet he's grown since I saw him last."

The talk continued over Molly, about the family, the friends in the area with whom Beverley kept in contact. Molly kept her gaze in front, watching the road, fascinated by her first sight of Texas. All the while, however, intensely conscious of Tell beside her, his body only inches away, his strong hands gripping the steering-wheel. Totally aware of the fact he hadn't seemed glad to see her.

What was wrong—did he think she didn't want Beverley to know? She felt guilty about their last night.

But she couldn't say anything now. Maybe when they were alone. Surely they'd be able to manage a few minutes alone.

Tell turned off the highway on to a secondary road. Soon he turned again on to a long black-top driveway, the wire fences on either side kept the grazing cattle from straying on the road. Molly watched as they drove into a large homestead, where a huge old-fashioned farmhouse with a wide covered porch stood in the middle. Behind it a hundred yards or more stood a barn.

There were cars parked every which way.

Tell stopped the truck and hopped out.

Opening the door for his aunt, he helped her down, then stood looking at Molly. She slid across the seat, her skirt riding up a little with the friction. She flushed and tried to pull it down. His hand caught hers and held it a moment, then tugged gently, helping her down from the high cab. Her fingers gripped his, but he pulled away.

"Beverley, so glad you could come."

A salt-and- pepper-haired woman hurried from the house and gave Beverley a big hug. "It's so good to see you again." She wasn't much taller than her sister. Turning, she gave Molly a bright smile of welcome.

"This is Molly Spencer, my secretary. Molly, my sister Sally Hardin," Beverley introduced them.

"Welcome, Molly. Tell, why don't you take Molly's and Beverley's bags up, show Molly her room? I'll catch up a little with Beverley."

His mother gave him a pat on his arm and moved with her sister to the front porch, already talking about the grandchildren and who would be at dinner that evening.

Tell pulled both suitcases from the back of the truck and climbed the few stairs to the porch.

"If you'll open the door, we'll go right up the stairs."

He waited for Molly to hold the screen door for him, then led the way. Molly followed behind him, feeling lost and overwhelmed.

The house was huge. She could see into the living room to the left and to the right a large dining room with a table that looked as if it could seat twenty. The wide stairs curved up to the right and she hurried after him.

He climbed the stairs leading to the second floor then walked down the hall to an open door. He placed Beverley's suitcase just inside the door. Then he continued down the hall to the last bedroom on the right. Pushing open the door, he entered and set her bag by the bed.

Molly followed.

"What are you doing here?" Tell asked in a hard voice as he straightened and reached around Molly to close the door.

Her heart began beating erratically, color rose in her cheeks. "You weren't surprised to see me?" She stalled for time.

"I knew you were coming. Mom's talked of nothing else for the last two days. More to the point, you weren't surprised to see me."

"Beverley told me who you were."

"I see."

Molly peeked up at his face, growing chilled at the hard look. "Tell?"

"What?" He stared down at her, his eyes slate-gray, a muscle jerked in his cheek.

"I'm glad to see you," she said in a small voice.

When he said nothing, her heart dropped. What had she done wrong?

Molly glanced around the room. It was pleasantly decorated in bright crisp cotton prints in southwest colors at the window and on the bed. The hardwood floor shone and the braided rug by the bed reflected the same colors from the spread.

She took a breath and looked at him again. "You said if I changed my mind to let you know."

"You were always to the point, Molly. You wanted a man with money. Is that why you're glad to see me now?"

"No." She stepped back, came up against the closed door. "I wanted to see you before I knew you had any money. I asked Miguel to let you know. He said you'd already gone. I... I sent a letter."

"Good try, Molly. No letter. How long have you known I was not the destitute cowboy you thought?"

"Beverley told me at the airport in Acapulco. But I'd already decided to come to Texas."

Molly was growing sick to her stomach.

Things were not going the way she'd thought they would. Tell looked at her as if he disliked her.

Where was the fun-loving, carefree man she'd known in Acapulco? The man who'd urged her to come away with him?

"So everything's perfect. You find the man with money enough to keep you secure and I get the girl, is that it?"

She shook her head slowly, staring at him with wide, frightened eyes. "You asked me to come with you," she whispered.

"Too right. I wanted you to come with me not knowing that I had any money. I wanted you to trust me, to want me for myself, not as a free meal ticket. It was important to me, Molly. I want to be wanted for myself, not because of money."

"I do want you for yourself."

"Since when?"

"Since before you left, all along, only I didn't realize it. Once you were gone, I knew how much I missed you, how much I loved you, how much I wanted to be with you, have you with me. I wrote you, days ago. Beverley only told me you were her nephew today."

"Seems too opportune to me," he ground out.

"It's the truth."

"I'll never know now, will I?"

"Ask Beverley, she'll tell you."

He gently set her aside and opened the door. In two strides entered the hall and left.

Molly stood where he'd placed her, shock rippling through. She'd come and he didn't want her.

He didn't believe she loved him, only that she wanted him because he had money.

The pain in her heart was searing.

Twelve

Molly heard Tell's footsteps as he walked down the hall, the hard heels of his boots hitting the stairs, growing fainter until she no longer heard him. The tears fell in earnest and she moved to the bed, sitting on the edge, her face in her hands.

He didn't want her.

After all was said and done, he didn't want her here.

Who would have thought anything could hurt like this? Her heart felt as if it'd break. That night on the boat when he'd told her he was leaving had been bad enough, but this was worse.

After everything, he thought she only wanted his money and he didn't want her on those terms.

She dashed the tears from her eyes, brushed her cheeks. Rising, she walked over to her window and looked out over the rolling land. She could see the cattle grazing in the afternoon sun. In the distance a tall windmill was silhouetted against the horizon. It was too far to see if it was stirring in any breeze.

It was her fault. She hadn't told him how she felt. She remembered Beverley saying women wanted him for his money. She didn't. She'd been ready to ditch all her long-held plans and beliefs to be with him when she thought he was some poor cowboy.

She should have said something long before today.

She looked back at the bed. She'd like to crawl in and cover her head and shut out the world.

But she couldn't. She was a guest in the house of Tell's mother and had to follow social conventions no matter how difficult it'd be.

She smiled sadly.

Manners were important to her, as he'd said, doing what was right no matter how she felt. Slipping off her jacket, she peered into the mirror. Her face looked blotchy and tear-stained.

Opening her door quietly, she peered out and saw the hall was empty. She found the bathroom across the hall and down two doors. She washed her face and applied make-up with a light hand. She had to venture forward, though she found it hard.

Would Tell be staying? Or would he return to his ranch now that he'd picked up the visitors?

She suddenly wanted to see him again. She didn't want him to leave before she could–

Could what? Get him to listen to her? Make him listen to her. In front of everyone who was around?

Molly slowed her pace. She couldn't do that.

Slowly she descended the stairs. Voices and snatches of conversations drifted in from the opened front door. People were gathered on the large porch. Shyly she pushed open the screen door and stepped outside.

"Come and sit over here, Molly," Beverley called to her. "We have lemonade or iced tea, whichever you prefer. Come and met my great-nephew. And the others."

Beverley motioned to one of several rocking-chairs on the wooden porch, most of which were occupied.

Molly smiled and walked over. Tell sat at the far side, balancing a young boy on his knee, rocking him back and forth and talking to him.

His eyes flicked to Molly and narrowed as he watched her cross the porch.

She sank gratefully into the chair beside Beverley.

"I'm Diane, Beverley's niece. And these wild kids are mine. The baby's Brandon, the young man with Uncle Tell is Thomas, and that sassy girl is Sue-Anne."

Tell's sister resembled him, with her dark hair and light eyes. She smiled in a friendly fashion at Molly. The baby was held so that Beverley could see him.

Sue-Anne was about two and talking a blue streak to her grandmother. Molly smiled and looked over to Thomas, who was having a wonderful time with his uncle.

Her eyes met Tell's again, and she quickly looked away. It was strange to see him in a family setting. Her thoughts of him had always been quite different.

"How did you like Acapulco?" Sally asked, handing Molly lemonade.

"It's a beautiful place."

"Boring, though, for a single girl who has to work there, I dare say," Beverley commented. "But Molly was good, she never complained."

"And were you bored?" Tell spoke from across the porch, his eyes boring into hers, the mocking light evident.

She took a quick sip of lemonade. How dared he bait her in front of everyone where she couldn't answer back?

If they were alone she'd tell him something that would make his ears burn. She glared at him and turned away before anyone else could see her expression. Schooling her voice, she said, "I wasn't bored. The work was interesting and I saw some of the sights in my time off. Met some of the local characters." Her voice was low, controlled.

"I'd hoped Luis would be able to show her around, but he needed to be in Mexico City. Molly only saw him a couple of times," Beverley explained to her sister.

"Old family friends, Molly. Did you like Luis?"

"Yes, he's very pleasant."

Old family friends—so had that been Tell at the party that night? Had he deliberately made sure she wouldn't see him there?

But why?

Was he ashamed to be with her? She was all right for a holiday fling, but not to acknowledge to his family or friends?

She felt Tell's gaze on her. But she refused to look his way, watching the ice cubes in her glass instead.

"I was sorry Luis was away so much. They went on the dinner cruise, but I was working so hard on the book that I guess I didn't allow for much time off for you, Molly," Beverley said.

"But I bet you honestly had a good time on the cruise with Luis, didn't you?" Tell's voice was silky.

She threw him a look and glanced away. He was being hateful. Hateful and hurtful.

"I enjoyed the evening," she said softly, not trusting herself to look at him, not wanting to remember that evening. She'd hated it when she'd learned he was leaving. That evening had changed everything.

"Trust me," Tell continued, setting little Thomas on his feet. "I'm sure any outing with Luis would be enjoyable. He'd give anyone a strong, secure feeling."

Molly flinched as if she'd been struck.

Why was he being that way?

She'd turned him down and when she'd changed her mind, as he had indicated she could, he refused to have anything to do with her. If he didn't want her, then why not just leave her alone?

"Tell?"

"Sorry, Mom. I've got to go. Things to do."

He rose and started down the shallow wooden stairs.

"Aren't you staying for dinner?"

"Another time. Goodbye, everyone."

His eyes skimmed the porch, held Molly's a moment, then moved on.

She watched him as he got into his truck, started it and drove off, gravel spurting from beneath the tires. She watched down the drive long after the truck disappeared from view.

Depression cloaked her and time seemed to stand still.

The rest of the afternoon passed like none Molly had ever known. The Hardin family drew her in as if she were one of them.

She played with the children, went with Diane when she changed Brandon, and when it was time for dinner she offered to help. It was the right thing to do.

All the women joined in to prepare the evening meal and Molly felt a camaraderie with the others that she'd never known while growing up. Everyone liked each other and the stories and conversations changed and flowed non-stop.

There were more people to sit at the table than Molly had ever seen at one family group. Jim Hardin, an older version of Tell, headed the table. Diane and her husband, Beverley, Tell's cousin Jack and his friend Marc, the children and Sally. These were the people he'd told her about in Acapulco. She felt as if she knew them already. She liked them. It was a lively group and Molly had no time to brood or worry about Tell.

Surprisingly, she was enjoying herself, though she wished that Tell had stayed.

Helping with the dishes afterward kept her from thinking.

She was pleasantly tired by the time the kitchen was put to rights. It'd been a long day for her.

The men drifted to the living-room, engrossed in a ball

game on the television. Diane had taken the kids upstairs to get ready for bed and Sally and Beverley settled at the kitchen table with coffee for a cozy conversation.

Molly wandered out to the porch. The night was still, the sounds of crickets in the background a soothing cadence in the warm night air, the soft murmur of the television a reminder of others near by.

The only illumination was that spilling out from the windows and the door. In the night sky, the stars shone with brilliance not seen from city streets. It was lovely.

In the distance, Molly could see the rolling hills give way to the star-studded sky. She leaned against the railing and thought of the view in Acapulco. This didn't compare, but it was pretty in its own way, enchanting, yet peaceful and serene.

She heard the step on the gravel at the side of the house and turned. Tell came around the corner, pausing when he saw her on the porch.

She smiled involuntarily, memory flashing back.

"The first time I saw you I thought you were a Mexican bandit," she said softly, remembering that first night.

He vaulted the railing on the side, and walked over to her, his boots sounding loud on the wooden porch.

"And I thought you were Aunt Beverley's uptight new assistant—trying so hard to get rid of the riff-raft." He stopped beside her.

Molly had to tilt back her head to see him. Her breathing was constricted. Her heart ached. Why had he returned?

"The view here's not quite the same," he said softly, turning to look out over the rolling fields and the star- studded night sky.

"No, but still pretty."

"Still pretty," he echoed and his head came down, blotting out the stars.

His lips were warm and gentle when they first touched hers, but soon they demanded, seeking and finding a response from her.

Only their mouths touched. Molly thought she'd float away. Every nerve-ending longed for him to wrap her in his arms, but she held herself away. The delight of his kiss made coherent thought impossible.

Tell's hands gripped her shoulders and gently moved her back, breaking contact.

She blinked up at him, disappointment flooding through her. Was he going to tell her goodbye again?

Leaning back against the railing, his legs spread apart, Tell brought her around before him, pulling her into the confines of his legs, his hands resting on her shoulders as he stared down at her in the faint starlight.

"I remember other nights in Mexico," he said slowly as his hand went to her blouse, slowly unfastening the top button, the second, the third. She thought instantly of the night in his tent. Her heart rate sped up. The dark shadow between her breasts was revealed, and he stared down at her, dropping his hands to hers, lacing his fingers through hers.

"I remember, too," she said, squeezing his hands. "I also remember wishing things had ended differently, that night. Now."

His face was in shadow, but she knew he was looking at her. She drew a breath and continued.

"This is all daring for me. I... I feel I threw everything over on a gamble. I don't usually gamble. And it looks as if I lost. Which is a good reason never to gamble," she said.

"What gamble?"

"I told you, I changed my mind. I wrote you to tell you. I didn't know you weren't a broke, drifting cowboy until the plane ride this morning, when Beverley told me. Ask her, if you don't believe me."

"So you were coming to me thinking I had no money."

He swung their linked hands slightly, Molly aware of every inch of his roughened hands against hers.

"You said to trust you. I thought about nothing else after you left. Life was miserable for me. I missed you. I wanted to spend time with you. See the laughter in your eyes when I said something you find funny. The nights seemed endless. I had trouble sleeping, but when I did, you were all I dreamed about. Life wasn't so good, so I could do one of two things. Get over you or take you up on your offer. I decided to trust in you, in us. Trust that you'd do the best you could for me, for us. You were right in saying I could make a living. Wherever I live there's always need for secretaries. So I wrote you," she said simply.

"Trust," he repeated.

"Yes."

She paused, trying to see him in the starlight. He hadn't left. He hadn't said anything either about wanting her to still be with him.

"I trusted in you. Can you trust in me? I love you. I risked everything I had in that letter—all my pride, my feelings. I can't help it if you didn't get it."

His hands tightened on hers and he slowly pulled her into his arms, his head resting on hers.

"I have to, Molly. I learned that this afternoon. When you got off the plane, clearly expecting to see someone and not a bit surprised when you saw me, I knew you knew I had money. You seemed so.. .so happy, like you'd found the gold at the end of the rainbow. I thought the money was the reason for your change. And the delight I felt seeing you made me angry. I was engaged once to a woman I thought was wonderful, only to find out a few months before the wedding that she was mainly interested in my money. Not me."

Molly's arms tightened around him. How could any woman not want him for himself alone?

"That's why I was so careful in Acapulco," he went on. "I wanted to be sure it was me, not anything else that attracted you. And all I got was how money was all you thought about."

"But it is you I want, Tell. I don't care about the money. Not any more. I just want to be with you, stay with you, love you."

"I realized that as today moved along I believe you sent a letter. I'll look forward to getting it when it gets here. Sometime mail from Mexico can take months. But I'm not waiting until then to say I want you. I wanted you in Acapulco, I wanted you when you got off that plane, and I still want you with a yearning that won't be denied. I love you, darlin". Stay with me forever. Marry me, and stay right here in Texas forever."

His kiss everything Molly loved.

Her heart soared and the happiness she felt threatened to explode. She saw stars, but were they from the dark Texas sky or the love of Tell Hardin? Her pulse increased as the blood raced through her veins. Her heart pounded or was it his? She was where she wanted to be, in Tell's arms.

When Tell pulled back, Molly longed for more kisses, for more explanations, to hear that Tell loved her.

But he took her arm and hurried her across the porch, down the steps and across the yard.

"Where are we going?" she asked, searching the barnyard in the faint light.

"My place. I want you for myself for a little while." His voice was low, rough with emotion.

"But what will everyone think?" she protested.

"They'll think you've gone for a walk or something. and I'll bring you back before everyone goes to bed."

"And tomorrow we'll tell everyone and start planning our wedding," he told her.

"Beverley's book. I have to help her finish it."

"She can do it here in Texas. You can help her with it as long as she stays here."

Molly smiled as he opened the door to the truck and helped her inside; he was taking over again. And this time she argue at all.

She slid across the seat to sit next to Tell as he drove through the dark Texas night.

"Lord, sweetheart, I've been miserable today. I thought you only came because you found out about the money."

"You don't think that any more, do you?"

She was anxious to clear that up. She didn't want that standing between them forever.

"No. I believe what you told me. I wish you'd told me before I left Mexico. Do you know what these last few weeks have been like?"

"Awful. I know because I lived through them, too," she said, snuggling closer, almost afraid to believe Tell loved her, wanting to touch him to reassure herself he was real.

"Do you want a big wedding?"

"No. I have no family, few friends. I'd just as soon get married quietly," she confessed.

"And quickly."

And quickly! Her heart sang.

Trusting Tell had proved the right thing to do.

As the truck raced swiftly through the night, Tell spoke again. "I kept hoping you'd show up, at the camp, or at the airport. I had to get back home, ranches don't run themselves. And I knew Aunt Beverley was doing okay. I didn't want to leave you behind. I had to know you wanted me, though. You always talked about money."

"I think I spoke more about security, not the money. It was only sort of about money. I hoped you'd come to the casita one more time," she admitted. "Every time I went on the patio, I looked for you. When I finally went to see Miguel, I couldn't believe you'd really left without seeing me again."

"Would your answer have been different?" he asked.

"Yes, if you'd come to see me again. A lot of the reason I changed my mind was because of the things you said."

"Hold on a second." He turned into another long driveway, stopping by the mailbox. Grabbing the stack in the box, he handed it to Molly, starting the truck again.

"I missed you so much. Everything I did or saw reminded me of you," she said. "Acapulco was no longer enchanting with you gone."

"I was angry at first that you wouldn't go with me."

"You didn't ask me to marry you, not then," she reminded him.

"I don't think I was thinking that far, only that I wanted you with me. I realized once I got home that I wanted you with me forever. I almost went back on the next plane."

"What if I hadn't come with Beverley?"

Molly was suddenly frightened at the thought of how close they had come to not being together, to not admitting they loved each other.

"I hadn't expected her before my mother told me yesterday. I planned to look you up in LA, see if I could fan the fire I thought was building."

She smiled and rested her head on his shoulder. The fire threatened to consume her. He had no need to fan it.

Tell stopped before a low, rambling ranch house, more modern than that of his parents. There was a veranda to the side and large picture windows which probably gave amazing views of his ranch.

"Do that cute trick where your skirt rides up when you get out," he suggested, the teasing light back in his gray eyes.

She laughed. With her skirt riding up and her blouse halfway unbuttoned, she no longer felt the same woman she'd been when she first met Tell.

He reached for her with a groan and Molly started to fall into his arms, but the flash of blue color from the corner of her eye stopped her.

She looked at the stack of mail. There, protruding from beneath a farm journal, was her letter.

"Tell, my letter."

She drew it from the stack and held it out to him.

"Look at the postmark. This'll prove to you I changed my mind before I knew about your circumstances, that I came for you alone."

He took the unopened letter and put it in his pocket, reaching for Molly.

"Thank you, darlin'", but I already knew that. Welcome home, Molly."

And he swept her into his arms and kissed her.

If you liked **Never Doubt a Cowboy**,
you'll love the next book in the *Cowboy Hero* series,
Cowboy Marshal.

If you enjoyed **Never Doubt a Cowboy**
please consider leaving a review.

More Books by Barbara McMahon

Cowboy Hero Series
The Cowboy Next Door
Cowboy's Bride
One Stubborn Cowboy
Crazy About a Cowboy
Never Doubt a Cowboy
Cowboy Marshal
Summer Cowboy
Second Chance Cowboy
Movie Star Cowboy

Cowboys of Wildcat Creek
Valentine's Cowboy Rescue
Shelly and the Cowboy
Kristi's Cowboy Hero
Holly's Reluctant Cowboy
A Cowboy for Eliza

Sweet Reunion Romance Collection
Unexpected Reunion
Unpredictable Reunion
Unanticipated Reunion

The Harts of Texas Series
Rebel Heart
Tangled Hearts
Reckless Heart

Sweet Romance Stand-alone Collection
Because of You
Cowboy Charade
I'll Take Forever
Jared's Promise
Mail Order Bride
Not Really Married
Sweet Meant To Be
The Cowboy Comes Home
The Paper Marriage
Trusting Jake
The Banished Bride